Country

DIAMOND MC
SEARCHLIGHT, NV

LILA ROSE

AUTHOR'S NOTE:

Country is book #1 in the Diamond MC. If you've read the MM Polished P & P series, you may have seen some of these characters. But you don't have to read them to enjoy *Country*. It will be its own standalone story.

Country, at chapter one, starts two years after West and Adrik's book.

PROLOGUE

Dusty

PAST

I stood in the compound with my heart in my throat as I looked around at all the men and women mingling. The women flirted so easily with the men. Envy flickered to life in my chest, wishing I had their skills. There was someone I wanted to approach, but my nerves were controlling me, and I couldn't get my feet to move from the floor, away from the wall I leaned against.

Still, my eyes stayed glued to the tall, wide man on the far side as he spoke with his biker club brothers. He wasn't the one who'd interviewed me for a position, but

I wished I had met him that day. At least I would have a name to put with the handsome face. His smile was radiant, his eyes soft and ones I could get lost in. His cropped dark-brown hair, where it was a little longer at the top, called for my fingers to run through it. I would have to get on my tippy-toes to achieve it, but I'd be willing to do so.

He threw his head back and laughed. A heavy breath fell from my lips, and I quickly bit down on my bottom one when I pictured myself kissing him right there on his tattooed neck. I even wanted to know what his neatly trimmed goatee and moustache felt like against my skin.

I probably looked like a stalking weirdo leaning against the wall and watching, and that was the only reason why I pushed off the wall and walked to the bar. As soon as I reached it, I sat on one of the few empty stools and rested my elbows on the top of the counter.

A guy around my age, or maybe a bit older, stopped in front of me. "Hey, what can I get you?"

"Um, a beer, please. But I, ah, don't have an ID on me." Why did I add that? Now I'd acted underage like I was at nineteen. Not that it didn't stop me from stealing out of my parents' liquor cabinet on the nights I was bored and extra lonely.

He grinned. "No need for one here. I'll grab you a beer." When he placed the bottle in front of me, we got to talking about random things, and before I knew it, I'd had another few drinks and was feeling slightly buzzed. I swung around on the stool with a giggle as I searched for the man who'd caught my attention. Even as I talked to Kylo, who was a prospect, I couldn't stop from searching out the man. I wanted to ask Kylo who he was, but the words died in my throat each time.

Though, with my spin on the stool, I couldn't find him anywhere, and my shoulders sagged at the thought of him leaving. It wasn't until I finished turning that I noticed a form close to my side. When I lifted my gaze, my eyes nearly bugged out my head, and I almost fell backward off my stool. *He* was there. Right there. He quickly reached out and took my arm, steadying me.

Once he saw I wasn't going to crash to the floor, his hand disappeared, and he smiled down at me. It was the first time in my life my clit pulsed from a smile.

"Ah, hey, hi, hello," I blurted, blushing. I glanced to the side to see if Kylo caught my stupidity, but he was serving someone else a drink, thankfully.

"Hey, darlin'." His voice was like a warm caress that hinted toward something orgasmic. If the sound was something to roll in, I would have got naked and jumped in. I couldn't believe he was standing right in front of me, and I was gaping like a fool.

Quickly, I snapped my jaw and waved, like I hadn't just told him hello three times in one sentence. His grin widened.

"You're new, yeah?"

"Uh-huh." I couldn't look away from him or form more words in my brain.

His chuckle had me wanting to tear off my panties and throw them at him. He took a sip of his beer, and there was that neck again, on show and waiting for my lips. I gripped the stool under me to keep from jumping at him.

"Dusty," I blurted when he'd looked away. I wanted his attention back.

"That your name?"

"Yep. Do you want a beer? I mean, I can buy you one."

He smirked. "Don't need to buy drinks here, babe, but I'll have one with you."

I wanted to palm my face. I forgot we didn't pay for drinks at the compound—all the booze was supplied. At least he wasn't running from how I'd acted. "I'd like that..."

"Country."

"Country," I muttered under my breath as he called out to Kylo for two beers after glancing at my empty bottle. I peered down to his thick tattooed arms and then to his vest, my eyes widened when I saw the patch read, President.

He was in charge of the club, and all I could think was that it would have to be a hard job to do since there were so many members.

Country passed the beer to me. When I took the

bottle, I tipped it his way. "Thanks. Can I ask you something?"

He nodded. "Yeah, Dusty." Oh boy, my name from his mouth sounded like porn.

"I… can't remember now."

He chuckled. "Then let me ask you somethin'."

Smiling, I nodded. I took a sip of the beer, kicking my feet since they didn't touch the ground.

His gaze made a quick run over me, and instead of feeling creeped out, I liked it. "How old are you?"

With a mock glare, I gasped. "You should never start with the age question."

His dark brow rose, and a chuckle sounded, this one softer. "I shouldn't?"

"No. Not unless you're prepared to answer it as well."

"All right, darlin'. You go first."

"Nineteen."

His eyes widened. "No shit?"

Shaking my head, I replied with his own words, "No shit."

"Babe" was all he said with a shake of his head.

"What?"

He rested his elbows on the counter and turned his head my way. "What you doin' here?"

Picking up my drink, I shook it a little. "Drinking."

"Nah, darlin', I mean what are you doin' at a clubhouse at nineteen? Don't you got better things to do? Go out with friends, people your own age?"

"No, I don't have many friends who I feel comfortable drinking with." Coffee dates, sure, but nothing where I felt I could let myself go and drink around them. I'd be too worried about what I'd say or do or if they found me annoying.

Yet, there I was drinking in a biker's club of all places.

Yeah, my actions didn't make sense.

My face heated. "I know it doesn't make sense because here I am drinking with you, but..."

"But?"

Shrugging, I took a sip of the beer and looked up at him. "I guess I feel safe here." Strange, even to my own mind. But I couldn't understand why, when I walked in there, I felt a sense of home.

He jerked his head back as if surprised by my answer.

"And don't think I didn't realize you didn't answer me about your age."

"I'm thirty-eight, babe." I didn't like the way his brows pinched together or the fact he looked away. I was sure my being younger was a problem for him.

"Um, I just wanted you to know that I don't think you're old."

He threw his head back and laughed. "Good to

know, darlin'. What made you join as a club girl, Dusty?"

"I overheard some women talking at a coffee shop about it." I pointed behind him. "Those two over there." He didn't look away from me. "I thought it was time to do something different in my life, and that decision took me here."

"No shit?"

Laughing, I shrugged. "No shit." It also happened to be at a time I was low and bored with my life.

He took one elbow off the bar and turned his body my way. My pulse raced when he reached out and tucked my light brown hair behind my ear. He caught the shiver it caused.

"You seriously don't care I'm way older?" He cocked a brow.

"No. Not at all."

"Good to know. Tell me somethin' about you, Dusty."

So I did, and we ended up talking for an hour, which included some light touches, knee bumps when he sat on his own stool, and many flirty smiles. It was the best fun I'd had in a long time, and I was glad I had those drinks to push my nerves back, as it meant I got to know Country and talk somewhat normally.

The crowded room had lessened a bit by the time Country stood from his stool. He gently pinched my chin to tilt my head back to have my gaze. My stomach put on a display of flips and twists. Was this where he was going to leave? I didn't want to see him go. I was enjoying my time with him. He'd made me laugh more tonight than I had in a long time.

"What do you want, Dusty?"

"P-Pardon?"

His eyes warmed. "Tell me what you want, darlin'."

"As in with my future or… tonight?"

He smiled. "Tonight, baby."

Baby. He said it in a way that had me feeling all soft inside.

With both hands, I reached up and gripped his inked wrist. I was going to take a leap. Take something I wanted from the moment I first saw him. "I…" I blew out a breath. "I'd like to go to bed with you."

His gaze darkened as he leaned in and kissed the corner of my mouth. His facial hair was rough, but I liked the way it tickled against my skin. "Then let's go to bed, darlin'." He took hold of my hand and led me through the compound and up some stairs to a room at the back. His room.

My hands shook from a jumble of nerves and excitement. When I heard his bedroom door close, I jolted and turned to him.

His brows rose as he watched my chest rise and fall rapidly. "You sure you want this, darlin'? You can walk out that door any time you want."

"No, I mean, yes, please." My face burned. "What

I'm trying to say is that… well, I couldn't walk out that door because I like where I am." *I want this. Please take me now.* His smile at my ramblings was a little smug, but I didn't mind. Even though it seemed my nerves were coming back.

"Fuck, darlin', you're somethin' special. I'm sure that's why the brothers didn't snap you up."

Or it could have been because they saw how I couldn't keep my gaze away from Country. Thankfully, the man himself didn't seem to notice my attention on him most of the night… before he approached.

Butterflies took flight inside me from knowing how lucky I was Country had come to the bar and stood beside me. If he hadn't, I would have gone back to my room dejected. When I'd first applied to be a club girl, Death, the man who'd interviewed me, made it clear the brothers would never force themselves on the girls. We had to be willing and wanting their attention.

Boy, did I want Country's.

He took a few steps to stop in front of me. My skin buzzed when he cupped my cheeks with both tattooed hands and slowly bent. His lips headed right toward mine, and I watched his eyes flick over my face, as if he was waiting for me to freak and stop this.

That wasn't going to happen.

His lips pressed against mine in a quick taste before he pulled back and caught my gaze. His touch wasn't enough. I *needed* more.

Lifting my hands, I slid them up under his vest and gripped his tee before stretching up for a better taste. When I tugged him closer and nipped at his plump bottom lip, he groaned and moved one hand to the back of my head. The kiss deepened. We opened to each other, exploring one another's mouth in a heated, hot kiss that had my toes curling.

Feeling brave, I dropped a hand to his perfect ass and took a handful that brought him in closer, where I felt his erection against my stomach. I wanted him in my mouth. Just thinking that had my body shivering and a moan slipping out. Country broke the kiss to clip, "Christ, darlin'." His heated gaze fell to my mouth, and he muttered, "Your mouth... fuck."

"C-Can I... I want to...."

His fingers threaded through the back of my hair and gripped, tearing a gasp out of me.

"Fuckin' beautiful. What you want, darlin'?"

"To suck you."

He groaned and rested his forehead against mine for a moment before his lips brushed against my cheek, my nose, the corner of my mouth. There he ordered gruffly, "Go sit on the edge of the bed." As soon as his hands fell away, I scrambled over to the bed and sat, looking up at him with my hands on my lap.

"Fuck me," he muttered with a smirk. I watched as he moved around the room, took off his vest, hung it on the back of a chair, and then removed his tee. His smooth, strong chest had my mouth watering. Across his chest was a tattoo, surrounded by others, of written words of the club's name. I wanted to reach out and trace them with my finger.

Later though, because as he started my way, he popped the button on his jeans. I rubbed my thighs together as my pussy pulsed. He slid the zipper down as he stopped in front of me. "Last chance, sugar. If you're havin' second thoughts, walk out. If you're not and want my cock in your mouth, then know this will be your only chance to go. As soon as this starts, I'm not gonna be able to stop."

"Country, I'm not going anywhere."

A growl rumbled out of him that had me running my hands up the back of his thighs to grip the top of his jeans and slowly pull them down. His cock popped free. The tip glistened with precum. He took himself in hand and held it out for me. When I went to dip in, he shook his head.

"Close your mouth, darlin'." I did, and my heart stumbled when he squeezed the base of his cock and brought his hand up his length, causing the tip to leak even more. He cupped the back of my head and rested his wet tip against my lips, running it over and around my lips.

He groaned, his chest rising and falling faster. "Fuckin' gorgeous. Open up now, baby."

I did and licked at the tip before flicking my tongue

around the head. Country made a noise in the back of his throat and jutted his hips forward, sliding his cock deeper into my mouth.

"Jesus, Dusty. I can't...." Wait, what? Panic started to ebb its way in, until he shifted back enough to bend, take hold of my tee, and pull it over my head. His hands were on my bra next, and his fingers were quick to undo it and fling it from my body. Next, he shoved my shoulder where I dropped back on the bed with a gasp, but I didn't mind at all, not when Country tugged my jeans and panties from me and threw them over his head as his gaze ran over my body.

Smiling, I now understood what he'd meant by he couldn't. He didn't want to wait. Already he was at the point of needing to be inside me, and I was more than willing to give him that.

"You've got me feelin' like a schoolboy, Dusty," he clipped through clenched teeth.

A laugh escaped. I covered my mouth, but he'd already heard it.

His brow rose. "You think it's funny?"

Pinching my thumb and finger together, I said, "A little."

Another growl sounded in the room as he grabbed my ankle and dragged me to the edge of the bed causing me to squeal. He bit inside my thigh, ripping a moan from my mouth.

"I'll have to punish you for laughin', darlin'."

Panting, I shook my head and looked down at him trailing kisses and nips inside of each thigh. "Can... can you do that later, please?"

He lifted his head. "Why, baby?"

Cupping my breast, I swallowed and told him the truth. "Because I need you inside me."

"Fuck. Fuck." He reached into his jeans pocket, grabbed his wallet, and pulled out a condom. I watched him rip it open and slide it on, and in the next second, he hooked my legs around his waist and pushed inside me. Arching, I cried out and wrapped my arms around his neck, needing him as close as possible.

"Baby, Christ, you fit me like a glove." He kissed my neck and slowly pulled out, only to return with a grunt. "Perfect. So fuckin' perfect."

"Country," I whispered before I sank my teeth into his shoulder. He groaned into my ear. His hips pulled back to slam into me, and I moaned around his skin, then licked the spot. "Yes, honey."

"Fuck, fuck, fuck," he muttered, sliding his hands down under my ass where he gripped, the speed of his thrusts increasing. I dropped my head back, panting and loving the way he filled me up, pressing me in all the right areas.

"God, yes." I glided a hand from his shoulder up and tugged on his hair. He gave me what I wanted by lifting his mouth from sucking on my neck to my lips. The kiss was long, slow, and amazing with the hard thrusts of his cock. My lower belly tingled. My pussy tightened around him, drawing out a grunted growl from him into my mouth. I drank it down and held him tighter. I moved my lips from him, panting out, "Close, honey."

He groaned, taking my lips in a wild kiss. I dropped my head to the bed and moaned, clamping around his cock as I came.

"Jesus, baby. You love my cock."

"Oh, yeah."

He cursed under his breath, then licked along my neck, biting my lobe where I heard the hitch in his breath and groan as he fucked me faster, filling the condom. He slowed his thrust, leisurely moving in and out of me until he stopped and looked down at me.

His gaze ran over my face, my breasts, and back up. When he had my eyes again, he grinned, and I couldn't stop the returning smile.

"Enjoyed that, darlin'."

"Me too."

"Good." He pulled out of me, and I *felt* the loss right away. Sitting up when he shifted away, I curled my arms around my knees and watched him get rid of the condom before doing up his jeans again. I wanted him again, but I could already see he was shutting that idea down when he pulled a new tee over his body.

It was then I knew my place. I was only a club girl, after all.

Quickly, I slipped off the bed and got dressed, ignoring the way disappointment twisted my stomach. I'd asked for this by joining as a club girl. It couldn't be any different between us, and really, I shouldn't have wanted it to after one night together.

I didn't know what the future had in store, but I would make it one where I was happy. Where I was welcome and not a nuisance.

Moving to the door, I glanced over my shoulder to see Country looking at his phone in hand with a pinched brow.

"Um, later."

He looked up, smiled, and lifted his chin my way. That was his goodbye. I took it because I wasn't there for something more. Well, that was what I would keep reminding myself.

CHAPTER ONE

Dusty

PRESENT

From the corner of the room, I watched as Country flirted with his new woman of the week, Rochelle. To me, it sounded like she was related to a roach. I hated her even before I met her. Pathetic, right? It wasn't like I was in love with Country. We'd slept together a couple of times, one before and then after his breakup with a different girl. Isla. Both of us had been a little tipsy each time.

So why can't you get him off your mind?

Shut up, stupid brain.

I didn't know why my eyes sought him out whenever I entered the compound. Or why my belly clenched when I caught other club ladies flirting with him, or why my heart turned into a wildly buzzing vibrator whenever he smiled or winked at me.

All right, I did know, but I wasn't going to let my little crush stick.

Not when I could save myself from hurt, since I knew, and I *definitely* knew, he was a player. He liked younger women, which I was, right along with a heap of other club girls.

I could have pussy punched myself for joining as a club girl when I didn't even need to. I didn't have bad parents. I didn't have someone to hide from or someone after me, as far as I knew. So why did I join? Because I wanted something different and exciting in my life, and when I'd first applied to become one of the club women in the Diamond MC—where I wouldn't sleep with anyone outside of the club—they promised I wouldn't have to have sex with every member. *I* could pick. That was two years ago, when I was a lot more nervous and shy, and the only member I had slept with was Country.

Why did I only pick him? Why did I feel that sleeping with someone else would be the wrong move? Especially when Country didn't care. He'd been with a few others.

Shaking my head, I took a sip of my vodka and cranberry and turned away from Country. I loved being in the compound. The atmosphere made me feel lighter on the inside. There were always people around to talk to, so I never felt lonely like when I went home to my parents' house.

Lonely had been my middle name for as long as I could remember. My parents loved me and always treated me well enough, but they were busy people. They explained they needed to work long hours because they wanted a future where they could retire without having financial worries. I understood. I did.

Rolling my eyes, I pushed them from my mind; it wasn't the time to think about how lonely I'd allowed myself to get. I had friends, but I didn't have anyone I ran to with my problems. It was my own fault for not opening up to people. The last thing I wanted was to be a bother.

Taking another sip of my drink, I looked to the bar and smiled. Kylo, or as his brothers called him, Gun, was leaning against the bar and walking two fingers up his husband's chest, Saint, with a flirty smile. I'd been surprised, like a lot of us in the club, when they'd gotten together, but anyone now could see the love they had for each other. My gaze snagged on another married couple. Wreck, who had always come across as a beefy asshole, was staring down at his husband, Lucas, while Lucas talked to State and Courtney, waving his hand wildly as he spoke. Wreck had shocked everyone more than Gun and Saint had. A few members weren't happy to have gay men in the club, but Country had put a stop to the complaints and said if anyone did have an issue, they could leave.

That was another reason why I'd stayed with the Diamond MC. I liked how Country ran things. He was fair but also stood up for things he strongly believed in —one was supporting his brothers and who they loved, no matter the gender.

"You seem to be thinkin' a lot tonight." Tech stepped up beside me with a smile. He took a drag from his beer, and I watched his throat move over the motion. Could I imagine sleeping with Tech? He was very good-looking.

Realizing he was waiting for an answer, I blushed and nodded. "Yeah, my mind's not my friend tonight." There were only a few members I felt comfortable and could be myself with. Tech was one of them, along with Country, though he did fluster me since I'd seen him naked. There were also Gun and Quake.

"Need a hand to get your mind off things?" Tech's smile grew flirty as he leaned his arm against the wall, facing me. Another great thing about the club was that when a woman said no, the men listened. Well, most did. There were only a few who tried to be persistent, but when their brothers yelled to knock it off, they did. They respected women, and I honestly felt safe in the compound.

The question I was fluffing around with was wondering if I could get my mind off Country by sleeping with Tech. With a quick glance across the room, where I saw Country kissing the roach on the cheek, I sipped my drink as my stomach clenched and looked up at Tech.

I cocked a brow. "What did you have in mind?"

His gaze ran over me slowly. "I could think of a few things."

He'd always been the biggest flirt with me, and I did enjoy his attention. I locked my eyes on his lips. Yeah, I could imagine kissing them.

"Would these things happen to be in private?"

"Definitely."

A shiver swept over me when he glided a couple of fingers over my cheek, and he gently brushed his thumb against my bottom lip.

Before his hand dropped, I sneaked my tongue out and licked over his thumb. His eyes darkened as he straightened.

"Dusty." My name was clipped off with desire.

"Just to confirm, nothing will change between us?" That was what I wanted most, because until I got over my... whatever it was with Country, I wanted to make sure Tech and I would stay friends.

"Baby, I ain't lookin' for anythin' long-term. Are you cool with that?"

"Cool as a cucumber." Okay, that sounded cheesy, but it had Tech chuckling, at least.

He nodded toward the hall where the bedrooms lay. "You wanna take a walk with me?"

I did. Didn't I?

I did because I loved sex, and I could use a little loving. Maybe even more experience would be good than having only two lovers. One had been my high school sweetheart, the other Country, and Lord knew I needed to move on from him, especially since he hadn't been looking for anything serious those two times I'd slept with him. I worked that out quickly when I'd woken in the morning and he'd pretty much said, "Thanks for a good night, Dust," and that was it.

Cocking my head to the side, I replied, "Depends." Reaching out my hand, I waited for him to take it.

When he did, Tech smirked and ran his thumb over the back of my hand. "On what?"

A shadow covered half of Tech's face, and we both looked to see Country standing there.

"Prez, what's up?"

Country crossed his arms over his wide chest. A chest I had seen naked. A chest I knew looked amazing. Still, Tech's could be just as good, and I had to give him a chance since the other man in front of me wasn't interested. Over his shoulder, I saw the roach stalking over. My upper lip rose, but I quickly took a sip of my drink.

"Need you to do somethin' for me."

Tech's eyes widened a little as he dropped my hand. "Now?"

"Babe, I slip off to the restroom for a second and

you're gone. What are you doing over here?" the roach asked as she wound her arms around his waist.

Jealousy uncurled inside me and bared its fangs. I stomped on the emotion, having no right to be anything with Country.

"Just dealin' with business, Chelle. Go grab us a drink, yeah?"

After she planted a claiming kiss to his cheek and glared at me, which was unnecessary, she swayed her hips over to the bar.

Straightening, I smiled at Tech when he looked my way. "I'll leave you both to it. When you're not busy, come find me." I poked him in the side and walked away. If I looked at Country, I worried he and Tech would see something I didn't want to show.

At the bar, as far away from the roach as possible, I placed my empty glass down and waited for the new prospect's attention.

"Dusty, settle something for me." Gun and Saint stepped up beside me. Over their shoulders, I caught another glare from the roach. What was her problem? I hadn't flirted with Country in front of her, and I tried to keep my gazes non-stalkerish. Did he tell her we'd slept together? If he did, he must have mentioned how long ago the last time was.

Six months, two days, and fourteen hours.

That's what I got for having a good memory.

Ignoring her, I smiled at the two men in front of me. "What do you need settled?"

"Prospect," Saint suddenly called. "Get Dusty the usual, yeah?"

"On it."

Gun clapped, and my gaze switched back to him after a grateful smile to Saint. "Right, tell Saint that you think it's better to give head than receive it."

It was lucky I wasn't drinking anything. I still gaped like a fish, not expecting that type of question.

"Wouldn't it be better to ask Wreck and Lucas or West and Adrik, since you all have to"—I leaned in to whisper—"suck dick, and it's different for me because I have a vagina, and I don't have a partner?"

Gun shook his head. "Doesn't matter about you having a pussy—"

"Poor girl," Saint muttered.

Gun and I stared at him. "You think I'm a poor girl for having a vagina?"

"Babe" was all he said, an amused glint in his eyes.

"I think I'm offended on her behalf." Gun smacked Saint in the stomach. "She's fine the way she is, even with her having a pussy."

We were starting to gain some looks, since Gun spoke loudly. My face burned, and I quickly took a gulp of my drink that the prospect placed on the bar.

"Can we stop talking about my vagina?" I urged frantically.

Gun winked. "Will do, as long as you answer the question. Do you prefer to give or receive?"

"You seriously want me to answer it?"

"Yes."

"But why?" It may have sounded a little whiny.

"Saint's a greedy bastard who likes to receive over give, but I'll forgive the douche if we get more people to agree with his side."

"And if I don't, then you'll be shitty at Saint for a while?"

Gun nodded. "Yes."

Grinning evilly, I clicked my fingers and pointed at Gun. "I'd rather give."

Saint snorted. "She's only sayin' it because she wants you pissed at me for sayin' what I did about her and her pussy."

"Oh my God, stop talking about my pu—vagina," I bit out in a low tone. "But seriously, I'm telling the truth." I did prefer to give a nice head job than receive one in return, as I always got shy when a guy was between my legs. I didn't understand why men enjoyed doing that to women when it was like an open wound down there.

Country sure liked it.

I didn't need that reminder.

I set my drink back on the bar and ran a hand through my light brown hair while Saint and Gun argued some more. Picking at a couple of strands, I pulled it up to look at it. My hair wasn't anything special, a boring color, really. I glanced over at the roach, who had her arm curled around Country's waist while he spoke with another member. I hated to admit it, but she had amazing long blonde hair that seemed full of life and not dull like mine.

Oh hell no. I wasn't comparing myself to her.

No way.

"Dusty, hey." Courtney stepped up with a smile and her one-year-old on her hip.

"Hi, Court. How are things?" She was State's woman, and they were set to get married in a couple of months. To me, they were the perfect couple. Courtney had been a godsend with the club girls. Since she became an old lady, the bitchiness was cut down, a schedule was made for cleaning and cooking, and she was so nice it hurt my teeth sometimes.

"Court, I have a question for you," Gun said.

"Abort. Run, Court, run." I gently shoved at her side, but she only laughed.

"What question?"

"Do you prefer to give or receive head?"

"Receive," she said instantly. "State does this thing with his tongue that—"

Saint covered her mouth. "Dear God, woman, we don't need to hear anythin' about State and his tongue. Especially not in front of young ears." He dropped his hand and turned to Gun. "Still, I appreciate your honesty." Saint crossed his arms over his chest and smirked at his husband.

Gun shot him the middle finger. "I'm gonna ask some more first." He quickly walked off and called out to Country. I didn't want to hear Country's answer, so I excused myself. When I didn't see Tech anywhere, I went up to the rooms supplied to the club girls and entered my own. I didn't have the energy to drive home to an empty house, knowing my parents would be either away on a trip for work or in their offices. I liked staying at the compound because there was always noise in the background.

I hoped Tech would finish whatever Country had him doing soon, and when he did, he'd come to my room. I had to move on. I had to let go of this infatuation and how it had controlled me for far too long.

The first step to get over him would be to sleep with another brother. If that didn't work, maybe, just maybe, it was time for me to move on from the compound. I worried I was sticking around here for all the wrong reasons. Like this place was the only way to fix my loneliness. Could it be possible I was going about things the wrong way? Was I supposed to be out in the world finding friends and dating someone who had nothing to do with the club?

Maybe.

CHAPTER TWO

Dusty

"Kill the bastard," I yelled, clicking the buttons on the PlayStation controller. "There, get him. He's right in front of you."

"I'm trying." Quake bumped my shoulder with his before his character died. "Fuck."

I groaned and slumped back on the couch. "You weren't fast enough."

"Babe, we've been at this game for hours. My fingers are going numb."

Snorting, I knocked my knee into his. "You're such a weakling."

He grabbed me and flipped me over his knee before smacking my butt. "Take that back."

"Quake, don't be," I said, laughing, "such a baby."

"Baby now? Baby? Right." His fingers dug under my armpits and tickled me.

"Shit, no, stop." My already full bladder was about to give. "I'll pee. I will," I cried, gasping for breath.

He paused. "You won't call me names when we lose then?"

"No... b—"

"Dusty," he warned.

"*Buddy*, I was going to say buddy. Now let me up, or I will pee all over you."

His hands released. "Yeah, I ain't into golden showers."

"Eww, me neither." I climbed to my feet and glanced at the clock on my wall. "Shit, I'd better get to work anyway."

"Guess it's lucky I got shot then."

"For once." I skirted around his grabby hands and went into the bathroom connected off my room, which I shared with another club girl who had her bedroom on the other side. After relieving myself, I walked back into my room and stopped.

Country stood in my doorway, and the conversation he and Quake were having died.

He tipped his chin up at me. "Dusty."

"Ah, hey. What's going on?"

"Just needed to talk to Quake for a second."

"Cool, cool, cool." I nodded. "I'll leave you two to it, since I've got to get to work." I grabbed my bag off the dressing table and started for the door, where Country stood. "Quake, get those fingers stronger for next time."

My face ignited when I realized how dirty that sounded.

Before I could fix it, Quake chuckled and said, "They'll be ready for you, babe. Have fun at work."

"Right, ah, yeah." Damn Country for making me flustered. I stopped in front of him since he hadn't moved out of the way. "Work. Got to get there. In the car. *Vroom-vroom.*" I blanched, shocked and a little sickened that I'd gone with car noises. Country's lips twitched while Quake, the ass, laughed. I ducked a hand behind my back and gave him the finger.

Country shifted to the side, and I quickly made my escape, but not before I heard Quake call, "Later, vroom-vroom." He wasn't going to let me live that down anytime soon. Great. It was Country's fault. I hadn't been close to him for a while, and his scent got into my nose, all but drugging me. He always smelled good. All male.

It'd been about a week since the night I nearly slept with Tech. I hadn't seen him since, and I wondered why. Was he super busy or dodging me for some reason? Did he regret hinting at a night together? Had I read into that conversation wrong? No matter what it was, I'd thought we were close enough that he'd say something or text, but nothing.

I could have asked Quake about him, as they were

good friends, but I didn't. Maybe I was scared what the answer was, since it seemed I had no luck in the bedroom department. Well, more that I couldn't keep a man around.

Still, I refused to let Tech eluding me get to me. When I saw him next, I'd smack him around the head a few times and tell him his chance to get in my pants was gone. I needed Tech and Quake in my life. They were good to have around and made the loneliness seem not as suffocating.

Pushing all of my confusion to the back of my mind, I walked through the front of the florist shop and smiled at Henri Duolle.

"Amour, you're late. Did you have a hot date?"

Pulling out my phone, I looked at the time. "I'm one minute late, Henri. How did you determine I was on a date? Not that I was."

"You're always early, and you don't have a life. I thought you got lucky."

"If you call hours of playing *Halo* getting lucky, then yes, I did."

His face screwed up. "That is *not* lucky, amour. It's bringing tears to my eyes with how boring it sounds." He shook his head and then brightened. "I know what you need."

"If you tell me I need cock—"

A throat cleared behind me. Henri smiled. "Mrs. June, it's lovely to see you."

"You also, Henri. Thanks for the call about the new roses in."

"Oh yes, of course. I'll go and get them for you." He quickly ran out the back and left me alone with a regular customer, who was in her seventies at least, *after* I used the word cock in front of her.

Turning to her, I gripped the strap of my handbag over my shoulder and smiled apologetically. "Mrs. June, I'm sorry about speaking like that."

She waved me off as she moved over to the lilies in a tub. "I was young once, and I did like the cock."

Did she just say she liked cock?

She hummed. "Though, no one is as good as my Bert. He might need a little blue pill to help, but he can still bring a smile to my face."

Was yelling *too much information* rude?

"Why, the other day, after he took the pill and went for hours, I was so sore I had to put an ice pack on my—"

"Here they are!" Henri shouted as he slipped through the swinging doors.

"Oh my, they're lovely."

"Oui, I couldn't agree more. Let me ring them up for you."

Good for Mrs. June for still getting some, but I didn't need to know that about a customer. How would I look her in the eyes next time when I knew she needed to cool down her vagina?

"Bye now, dear," she called to me on the way to the door. Meanwhile, I was still frozen in the same spot.

"Bye, Mrs. June."

"Good luck on finding some cock."

"Ah, thank you?" As soon as the door closed after her, I turned to Henri.

He looked a little pale. "I couldn't let her finish speaking of her—" He gagged and shuddered dramatically. "I've always been scared of ladies' lower bits."

Snorting, I shook my head and walked around him to the back, where I would put together the afternoon orders for deliveries. "It's a good thing you're gay, then."

"It sure is, or I'd be living as a monk right about now."

Shaking my head, I shooed him back out the front. "Leave, or I'll get nothing done."

Luckily, we heard the front door open, and he did disappear, or he would have gone back to telling me what I "needed." I didn't need anything except maybe a lesson on how to speak normally around Country.

An hour later, I still couldn't believe I'd said vroom-vroom. What was I? Five years old?

"Henri," I called.

"Oui, amour?"

"I'm heading out back to load the van."

"Keys are on the file cabinet in the office."

"Thanks." I grabbed the first bouquet of flowers and

the keys before heading out the back door to Henri's van. As usual, I winced when I spotted the vehicle. I'd lost count of the times I'd told him to change the signs on the van since it looked like a dick entering a vagina instead of flowers with their stems.

Huh, maybe that was why dicks and vaginas were on my mind recently. I'd definitely spoken about them enough for a while.

I quickly finished stacking the flowers and made my way back inside for the last time to grab my bag. "Henri, I'm off."

"I know. I can smell you from here." He laughed at his own joke as he slipped into the back area.

"You need a man, Henri. Then he might be able to teach you how not to make terrible jokes."

"Non, amour, you need a sense of humor. I'll be here when you get back."

"Don't work too hard."

"When do I ever?" He winked.

"All the time, and you tell me I have no life."

"Go out with me then."

"To a gay club?"

He shrugged. "Any. I'm not picky, and I do a good job at sucking straight men's cocks who want to live on the wild side for the night."

Groaning, I palm my face to hide my smile. "You're terrible. But I'll think about a night out." With a wave, I made my way back out to the van and climbed in.

Starting the engine, I pulled my sunglasses out of my bag and slipped them on with a smile still on my lips. I'd only been working with Henri for a couple of months, and I already loved it. He was busier than a lot of the florists around town. The previous place I got fired from, since the owner's new wife didn't like me, was on the other side of town, but he'd never been as busy as Henri's.

I could see why.

He didn't have the charm that Henri had.

I wasn't the only employee at Henri's. He had a morning guy who did deliveries. Only Henri and I put together bouquets, and I was only allowed since I'd proven I had the skills with colors and arrangements.

Flowers had always been a passion. My parents' yard was the talk of the street. I had spent so much time getting it just right, making sure I grew an abundance of flower varieties so I could cut and arrange them. I had a nice Instagram account, a portfolio of sorts, where I posted photos of my work using the flowers from my parents' yard. Showing my account to Henri was the reason he'd given me a chance, since I didn't have a degree to go with it.

God, I really did need a life.

Still, I didn't see a problem with enjoying my work. It was better than my other job. I worked three late-night shifts cleaning a veterinary clinic. I needed all the money I could get. While it was good to stay at the compound, I wanted a place to call my own, without my parents' help.

I would have enough for a mortgage deposit in another year if things stayed on track.

By the time I was done with the deliveries and letting Henri know it'd have to be the weekend to go out, I drove back to the clubhouse and went right up to my room, knowing I had a pile of laundry to get done. Not only my things, but I did it for several members of the club. It made me feel better to help, as I did stay there rent free, like all the club girls. It was why I also spent most Sundays preparing as many meals as I could for the week for the club. The other nights the brothers had cookouts, called for pizza, or got another club woman to make something, since none of their members were any good in the kitchen.

Slipping through the bathroom, I knocked on the other bedroom door and slid it open when Stracy called out.

"Hey." I smiled as she waved at me, throwing me a wink too.

My smile slipped when I took in the person sitting on the end of her bed, filing her nails. Davina glared at me. She was a newer club girl and wasn't picky when it came to the brothers.

When she sucked in a breath, I knew she was about to spit some shit my way. "You know you getting a room here is bullshit, right? You don't even fuck any of the guys."

"Davina, she's been here longer than you, and the guys like her," Stracy put in from where she sat, leaning against the headboard while painting her toenails.

Davina snorted. "Bitch, I'm nice *and* I suck cock. She shouldn't get a room here because she doesn't open her legs. Instead, everyone knows she only hangs around here because she's pining for something that won't ever be hers."

My throat thickened as I took a step back. Was that how all the girls thought of me? I pulled my weight around here to make sure I didn't have to sleep with just anyone. But I didn't realize my little crush was obvious to everyone.

Even though I wanted to slap the bitch or knock a few teeth out, I ignored her. What could I say to that? "Stracy, do you have any washing?"

Davina cackled. "See, she can't even defend herself because she knows it's true." Her smile was sarcastic. "Honey, do everyone a favor and pack yourself up. Country doesn't want you. He's too busy fucking real women. It's obvious he feels sorry for you, to keep letting you stay here."

"Davina, enough," Stracy snapped.

But it was too late, her words already burned inside my mind, and I was too weak to stop them hitting their mark.

"Come on, Strace, you see it. We all do. Hell, she even made a pass at Tech, and he's been ignoring her since. All the girls are talking about it."

Grinding my teeth together, I left the room, not willing to listen to any more. Closing the door on my side to the bathroom, I slumped against it. I was already thinking how stupid I was, yet I didn't know everyone else thought the same.

But I paid my way to have a room here by helping out instead of fucking anyone with a dick. I didn't stay here to sponge off the club.

Is she right? Does Country let me stay here because he feels bad?

Fuck.

Her words simmered inside me, and I was afraid that a part of what she said was true.

CHAPTER THREE

Dusty

*I*t was Saturday, and I was in the kitchen with both hands in a mixing bowl as I combined the second batch of cookie dough; I already had the first batch, along with some other goodies in the oven. I was cooking today instead of Sunday, because I wasn't sure what type of shape I'd be in after a night out with Henri.

Rough laughter filled the area before the doors opened, and Tech, with Country, stepped through.

Stilling, I pulled my gaze back down to the bowl before they saw me looking. It didn't stop my heart from skipping a beat while my belly dropped to my feet.

"Hey, Dusty," Tech called.

Nodding, I rolled the dough into a ball and placed it on a tray. "Tech."

"Woman—"

The doors opened again, and, of course, it had to be Davina, along with Abi. As soon as the girls saw their prey, they swayed over to the guys and curled around them. Davina to Country, while Abi ran her hand down Tech's chest.

"Hey, handsome. Thanks again for last night," Davina cooed.

I swallowed the rising vomit and went on rolling the dough. My hands shook a little, and I glared while cursing under my breath.

"No problem, Davi."

No problem, Davi. I'll take you to bed anytime, Davi. Your pussy is so sloppy it sounds like mincemeat, Davi.

"Tech, you look a little stressed. How about I help you relax?"

Gag. Abi was laying it on a little thick. Then again, most of them did when they wanted something.

Chancing a glance at them, I saw Country's hand on Davina's hip, and Tech's was the same on Abi. They weren't pushing them away. They weren't telling them they'd catch them later. They wanted their attention.

These cookies had looked good, until now.

While the women whispered sweet nothings into the guys' ears, I finished the last ball, glared at all the people, and sucked the extra dough off my middle finger, meeting Davina's gaze.

What I wanted to do was pick up the tray and smack it into the bitch's head.

"Not into it, woman." Tech gently set her back, and she left with a huff.

"Maybe later, Davi," I heard Country say just as Quake walked into the kitchen.

"Quake," I yelled.

He froze in the doorway and eyed us all. Did he just sigh? He started forward again until he was by my side.

"What you got there, Dusty?" He looked into the mixing bowl, then the cookies, and I was sure his gaze glazed over.

"Want a taste?"

His gaze swung up to mine, and I cocked a brow. He leaned in and whispered, "Was that innuendo or something else?"

My head jerked back. Quietly, I asked back, "Did you want it to be?"

Still low, he said, "I don't think I do. I like what we have."

Nodding, I uttered, "And I'm okay with that, but since you're knocking me back, you have to flirt with me when I say."

"Why?" he clipped softly.

"Because I said so, and friends help each other out."

He sighed again. "Fine. As long as I get food out of it."

"Fine." I grabbed a rolled dough ball and brought it

to his lips. He started to glance back at the others until I bit out, "Don't." I shoved the ball into his mouth, a little harder than necessary, and kicked him in the shin. He groaned. That kind of sounded like he was turned on. Maybe. I needed to flirt more to know if I was doing it right.

"How's that taste?"

Quake glared as he nodded and hummed under his breath, still chewing. "So good."

Smiling, I patted his arm and turned to the oven, taking out the cinnamon rolls to place the cookies in.

"Country, can I ask something?" Davina cooed.

"Sure."

Facing Quake, I glanced over his shoulder, only to quickly look away when I saw Country and Tech watching us. The only one smirking was Tech, but what did he have to smirk about?

"Aren't all club girls supposed to... please your men?"

Oh, she wanted to play dirty. Opening my mouth, I went to retort but then snapped my mouth closed when I realized it would be bad sinking as low as her.

"We never force anyone, Davi. You know this." Country's tone held an edge, but it could have to do with being questioned like that in front of people.

"Can I have some of that?" Quake asked. Davina whispered something in Country's ear.

I didn't have to stick around to see this. Though,

maybe it was better for me. Maybe watching him hold, kiss, and fuck other women would help me get over this stupid little crush.

Country's brows lowered, and his lips thinned to whatever Davina was saying.

"Dusty?" Quake said.

"Huh?" I pulled my gaze up to his.

He pointed at the cinnamon rolls. "Can I have one?"

Shaking my head, I grabbed a bowl of icing. "I have to put icing on them when they cool. But you can have a muffin. They're in a container in the pantry." Quake quickly moved over to the walk-in pantry. I heard a moan from within.

"Dusty." Tech had moved up to replace Quake beside me. "Gotta tell you, babe, it's good to be back home to your baked treats."

"Back home?"

"Yeah. Didn't someone tell you I had to slip off for business?"

"No." I grabbed the wooden spoon from the bench. "But you could have called or texted or something." I cringed at how clingy it sounded. He wouldn't understand that the ladies had been talking.

Frustration had me snapping the spoon across Tech's knuckles when he reached for the icing bowl. "Jesus, woman. That hurt."

It would, and I was sorry, but I didn't voice my apology, too busy being pissed at myself for caring what everyone thought of me. Tech and I were friends. He didn't owe me anything. I only got butt hurt because of the gossip.

Angry tears welled. I had to get out of there so I didn't slam that bitch's head into the counter, since she wouldn't quit whispering.

Fuck her.

Fuck him.

They could fuck each other for all I cared.

The door opened again, and when I looked that way, I noticed Country gently ushering Davina toward the doors as Courtney and Eve walked in.

"There she is." Eve grinned. She skipped over and smacked her brother, Tech, in the back of the head before shoving him out of the way. "Dusty, what are you doing tonight? Court and I were going to have a girls' night."

Tech groaned. "Don't do it, Dusty. They'll drag you into nothing but trouble."

The buzzer on the oven shrilled, and I quickly turned to take the first batch of cookies out.

"Smells like heaven in here." Gun had appeared with Lucas and West. The kitchen was big, but it was starting to get crowded.

"Drop the muffins, big man, and step out of the pantry." Eve stood at the mouth of the pantry.

My eyes widened, and I stalked around the counter to the pantry entrance and gaped. "Are you shitting me, Quake? I had half a dozen in that container, and there's only three left." I snatched the container of muffins out of his hand and turned.

I stilled when I looked up into Country's amused gaze. He reached in and took a muffin before winking and stalking out the kitchen.

"You'll make more, right?" Quake asked.

Glaring over my shoulder, I placed the container on the counter. Gun and Tech quickly grabbed the last two. I huffed. "I'll make more. Just none for you, Quake."

"Dusty, I'm a growin' man. I need all the food I can get."

Eve snorted. "You stopped growin' ages ago." She shoved in beside her brother again and curled her arm around his waist.

"Back to Eve's question," Courtney said as she eyed the cooling cookies. "Mom's having Crispin for the night. It means I can drink, since I pumped all the breast milk I could out of me, and I'll do it again in the morning to get rid of any traces of alcohol." She cupped her breasts, and I noted the men in the room quickly averted their eyes. "They'll get tender, but it'll be worth it. I haven't been out for ages. Please tell me you can come, Dusty."

Tech snorted. "Yeah, Dusty, can you come?" Eve elbowed him in the ribs, causing him to grunt. "I was kiddin'." He smirked at me. "Or was I?"

I picked up the wooden spoon again, and he took a step back. I moved into him, and while the others talked about what a night out would entail, I whispered to Tech, "You had your one and only chance to get into my pants. It's not happening again. We stay friends without benefits."

He clutched his chest. "You wound me, Dusty. I asked Country to come tell you I was gonna be out of town. I don't know why he didn't, and I'm sorry I didn't call or text, but shit got busy, and I had to focus."

Why hadn't Country said anything?

Thinning my lips, I shook my head. "Sorry, Tech, but I think it's for the best. For now. No, I'm pretty sure it is."

He tapped under my chin, and I brought my gaze up to his. "If you ever change your mind, I'll leap at the chance, Dusty. But I get it also. We're good friends."

Smiling softly, I nodded. "We are."

"You also cook for us, so I can't risk you gettin' too attached to me."

Scoffing, I shook my head. "You'd be the one getting attached."

He cocked a brow. "Babe." He gestured to himself and smirked.

Groaning, I moved back to the counter where the cookies were now on a plate, and people were eating them. I'd have to make more.

"Eve, how do you put up with a brother who thinks so highly of himself?"

"I give him a mirror to entertain himself with, and then I don't see him for hours."

"Wench," Tech coughed into his hand.

"Douche," Eve said with a roll of her eyes. "Now, back to the night. Gun, West, and Lucas are in. You up for it, Dusty?"

"Actually, I have plans tonight to go to a club with my boss from the florist. Though, I do appreciate the offer." I really did, because I thought highly of Eve and Courtney. They weren't club girls. They didn't owe me anything, since I was one, but they always seemed to be nice to me, and Eve wasn't pleasant to many people. She told me once that she had a short fuse for stupid people. I was honored I wasn't classed as an idiot like she obviously thought the other club girls were.

"That's all right. You mind if we go to the same club?" Eve asked.

"Not at all, and I'm sure Henri would love to meet people in my life, since he thinks I don't have one."

"He doesn't know you hang around here?" Gun asked.

"No. I don't tell anyone anything about here. It's none of their business."

"Are you sure your boss will be all right if we go as well?" Lucas asked. He was such a sweetheart.

"He'll love it." I smiled.

"You do realize somethin', right?" Quake asked around a mouthful of cinnamon roll.

"Quake," I snapped and threw the spoon at him. His head rocked back, and he rubbed his forehead, glaring at me while others laughed. "They weren't finished. I'm going to be *here* all night if you keep eating everything."

Courtney patted my hand and smiled. "We'll help you get some more stuff out to make sure you can make it." I returned her smile, my chest suddenly warm.

"Thanks."

"I'll help by watching. I'm not the best cook." Eve frowned.

"I'll teach you if you want," I offered. "I usually bake every Sunday. You can join me any time you want."

"That'd be cool, Dusty, thanks."

"Can we go back to what I was sayin'?" Quake said, licking his fingers clean.

"What?" West asked.

"How you guys aren't realizin' it won't be just your group at the club."

"What are you talking about?" Courtney asked.

He pointed at West, Lucas, and Gun. "If these three are goin', you know their other halves aren't gonna let them go solo."

West shook his head. "I'm sure if I asked Adrik to stay home, he would."

We all looked at him and laughed. West rolled his eyes but smiled softly, obviously thinking of his possessive Russian man.

The door swung open. "We'll sit away. You won't

even know we're there," State said as he walked over to Courtney and wrapped his arms around the front of her. Wreck, Adrik, and even Saint also claimed their partners in some form of touch.

I wished I had that.

"Honey, you're not going." Courtney stamped her foot.

Tech slapped Quake's back while they both chuckled. "Too bad we've got to work tonight. I'd have gone just for the show."

"Wait, there's a show where we're going?" Lucas asked. We all stared at him before laughing. Though, his man wasn't. Instead, he kissed the side of Lucas's head.

"Tech just thinks there'll be trouble they'll miss tonight," I said to Lucas.

"Oh." He nodded his understanding.

Eve clapped. "All right, boys. Out of the kitchen, and the plan is to meet out front at seven. I'll get the details off Dusty on where we're going and send a group text. Now shoo." It didn't surprise me they all listened. No doubt they had things to do, but some might also be afraid to get a wooden spoon to the head.

Excitement unfurled in my belly. Suddenly I was looking forward to my night. I was glad Henri had suggested it, but also that Courtney and Eve had asked me about my plans.

Maybe I did have friends after all, and I hadn't realized. But would they be the type to share everything with?

Would they judge me over my small crush?

They seemed the type to support you no matter what, and maybe they'd give good advice on what to do.

Though, I doubted it would be a good time to speak of it while drinking. There was also a chance I was leaning on them too soon. Groaning inwardly, I went about cooking and thought about why I was so socially awkward and didn't know shit about having close friends.

Of course, it had to do with how shy I had been, but in the last two years, I thought I'd changed. Grown. No matter, I liked who I was now. I liked the people in my life, and I didn't want to lose them or what I had.

CHAPTER FOUR

Dusty

$\mathcal{T}$he music was pumping as we walked into the club. The crowd parted for us, but I was sure it had to do with Wreck and Adrik at the front of the group. Both were unsmiling, big, and gruff. If I didn't know the men, I probably would have peed myself a little at the sight of them.

Henri stood at the bar, looking out to the dance floor. With Courtney and Eve at my sides, I made my way over. Henri spotted me, then the others, and his eyes widened.

"Hey, boss." I smiled, stopping in front of him. But he was busy scanning my group. "Henri?"

He leaned into me. "Please tell me at least one of the men is single and gay?"

Laughing, I shook my head. "All taken, sorry. Henri, this is Eve, Courtney, Gun, Adrik, Lucas, Wreck, Saint, and West. Guys, this is my boss, Henri."

Henri's gaze didn't move from West. In fact, I was sure I saw a little drool at the corner of his mouth. He shifted closer to West with his hand held out. "Bonjour, mon amour. You are just delicious."

West chuckled uncomfortably and took Henri's hand, until Adrik placed his hand over theirs. "You do not touch him."

Henri swallowed and blinked up at Adrik. He nodded slowly and dropped West's hand.

"Adrik, it's fine," West tried.

"Nyet, it is not. Already I hate this place with the number of eyes on you."

West wrapped his arms around Adrik's waist. "But you're the only eyes I care about."

Adrik's lips twitched. "Good answer, moya lyubov'."

"Oh my," Henri breathed. "Dusty, you didn't tell me how many goodies you hang out with. I thought you were boring." He winked at Gun. "What about you, honey? Wanna walk on the gay side?"

Saint curled an arm around Gun's shoulders. "He already does."

Henri groaned and shifted his gaze to Lucas. "Please tell me—"

"Don't fuckin' think about it." Wreck's rough tone jolted Henri back a step.

"I told you they were taken."

Henri sighed. "I had to try." He whimpered when he watched Wreck smile down at Lucas. "You have to tell me how you know these people."

"I will. Let's get a drink and a table."

"I don't think everyone would fit into a booth, unless someone wants to sit on my lap?"

"Nyet."

"No."

Saint chuckled and shook his head. "Give it up, man. It ain't happenin'."

Henri sighed and nodded. "Drinks then."

Patting his arm, I turned toward the bar. After we all ordered, we moved over to the left side of the club, where booths lined the wall. Only none of them were free… until they saw Wreck and Adrik, and suddenly two came up available. Henri and I shared a look.

He leaned into me. "I'm getting a boner from just watching their dominance."

"Too much information, Henri."

"Please, you can't say you're not wet from—"

"Henri," I clipped. "No. They're friends." Why did it feel so good to say that? "Get in the booth." I nodded toward it. Henri slipped in. I followed, as did Courtney and Eve. Gun went to slip in the other side, where he would be sitting next to Henri, but stopped when Saint pulled him back.

"Eve, do me a solid and sit next to Dusty's boss."

Gun laughed. "Saint, I'll be fine."

"No offense, but I can already tell he'll have wandering hands."

Henri cackled. "Too true, mon amour."

Eve rolled her eyes and shifted to Henri's other side. Gun sat next to Eve, then West and Lucas took up the last seat by Courtney.

The other men moved to the booth beside ours and slipped in.

"I do love how cozy this is. It's like the start of our own little gang bang."

Gun groaned. "Why am I at the women's table?"

"This is where the fun will be," Henri supplied before turning back to me. "But seriously?" He glanced to the other booth. "Do they have any friends who are gay or I can switch?"

"I'm afraid not."

Henri pouted. "It's like my glitter rainbow just crashed to the floor." A guy walked by the booth. "Well, hello there, mon amour." He winked, and the guy flushed before he kept going. I guessed he wasn't too devastated. "Tell me, how do you all know my Dusty?"

Everyone looked to me. I took a gulp of my drink and coughed.

Eve shrugged. "She's been hanging around us for two years now."

"We're slowly getting to know her." Courtney smiled.

Eve laughed. "Yeah, when she lets us. I always thought you hated us."

Scoffing, I shook my head. "Me? No way."

"You stick to yourself a lot." Lucas offered a gentle smile.

"I've always talked to her." Gun winked my way. That was true. I always found it easy talking to Gun when he was a prospect for the Diamond MC. I still did. It was just harder these days, because everyone was busy with other things in their lives.

"I… I never wanted to be a burden." I sucked back the rest of my vodka and added, "It's… I don't know, something I've always hated. That if someone didn't want me around and they didn't say anything, then I wouldn't know, and I'd be pushing myself on them."

They stared at me.

"Dusty, how could you ever think you'd be a burden?" Courtney asked. "You're the only girl I like at the club, besides Eve. And you're the only one who smiles naturally at the guys, as if you count them as friends, with no hidden agenda. The only one who puts themselves out there to help. You're kind, sweet, and good-natured. You've never been a burden."

My heart melted into goo, and I had the sudden urge to hug Courtney, so I did. "Thank you," I whispered.

"What club are you talking about?" Henri asked.

Sniffing, I turned to him. "I'm a club girl for the Diamond MC."

His mouth dropped open, and his eyes rounded as he made a noise in the back of his throat.

"I'll go get us more drinks," West offered.

"I'll help," Lucas said, and both slid out. When they headed toward the bar, they were soon followed by Adrik and Wreck.

"You're not boring at all, amour, are you?"

Shrugging, I waved a hand in front of me. "I think I still am. Even though I joined for some excitement in my life."

Henri gripped my hand. "Wait, wait, wait. Doesn't being a club girl mean you sleep with the bikers?"

Groaning, I used my free hand to palm my face. "I think I need more drinks before I say any more."

"Oh, this is going to be good. Move it, Gun, I'm going to get shots." Eve shoved at Gun, who chuckled and got out of the booth. Of course he disappeared to Saint's side. I didn't know if I could talk about Country or if I was supposed to, but either way, I still needed liquid courage.

"I LOVE THIS SONG," I cried and wiggled in the seat. "Who wants to dance?"

"Soon." Courtney smiled. While I waited, I lifted my

hands in the air and waved them around while singing, probably poorly.

"Come now, amour, earlier you were going to tell us about the men at the club."

I blinked slowly at him. Were there two Henris? Since when did he get a twin?

"Men? Noooo," I drew out. "There was only one. One mouth-watering man I had a taste of, and now I can't get him off my mind. But he doesn't want me. Okay, he might want my vagina." Groans sounded around me. "But nothing serious because he doesn't just like my vagina. He likes many." I dropped my forehead to the table, and someone patted my head. "I'm not worthy of his awesomeness anyway. He'll find his old lady eventually, and I'll be... sad. I will be. I can admit that, right? You guys won't say anything." Did I just screw up and say things I wasn't supposed to? Damn alcohol brain.

"Our lips are sealed, babe."

I lifted my head and smiled at Eve. "You're awesome. I nearly slept with your brother, but I'm glad I didn't, because he's cool, and so is Quake. They're good friends. Though, if Quake doesn't get better at *Halo*, I'm going to have to rethink about him."

Eve grinned. "I'll let him know."

Nodding, I picked up my drink and took a sip. "Why is this water?"

"It might be good to drink some," Lucas said.

"You're cute." I leaned across the table and pinched his cheeks, then rubbed my palms against them. "So cute, but don't tell Wreck I said that. He'll kill me."

Lucas smiled. "I won't tell him."

A chuckle next to Lucas caught my attention. "West. Hi. Hey. You're cute too. Where's Gun?"

"He left with Saint, remember? They're heading to work so State can come here for Courtney."

"Courtney? Where is she?"

"Right here, babe," Courtney called. She stood, hips swaying, hands in the air, just outside the booth.

"We're dancing!" I pushed the water to the side, gripped the edge of the table and slid my body over it. I would have tumbled to the ground if hands hadn't grabbed me. The world spun as I was lifted to my feet. "Adrik." I grinned up at him. "You know you're scary, right? But you're also cool because you take care of West, and West is amazing. Not that you're not amazing, because you are. In a killer kind of way."

"I am unsure if I should say thank you."

Beaming, I patted his chest. "You're welcome." Wow, his chest was really hard. I glanced around for West. "You're a lucky, lucky man."

West laughed. "I believe so. Though, I would prefer if you stopped running your hands over him?"

I pulled my hands back like they were on fire. "Oops, sorry. All that's West's."

"Da, it is."

"Dusty, come dance with me." Courtney wiggled her fingers, and I took her hand. She pulled me close, and together we danced and sang. Friends kept passing us water to drink as they mingled around us. It wasn't until sometime later that we stopped when Courtney was pulled out of my grasp.

Looking over her shoulder, I saw State, who grinned at me before saying something in Courtney's ear. She turned in his arms and kissed him like he was breakfast, lunch, and dinner.

Movement beside State caught my attention. I looked there, and my heart buzzed inside my chest.

Country.

Handsome Country stood to the side, talking to a waitress and Wreck. Country laughed at something the waitress said, and my belly dropped down to my feet with a whimper. I liked his laugh. I'd managed to get a few laughs from him the nights we'd been together.

I wanted more nights.

I wanted more than just nights.

But I couldn't, because, well, he wasn't mine. He didn't see me as his old lady, and I couldn't, wouldn't change who I was from whatever Country saw lacking. I liked who I was. I'd come out of my shell and was comfortable around the club, yet he still didn't see anything in me to deem me interesting.

It sucked. It really did.

But I couldn't change his mind about me.

Country's gaze settled on me. When he smiled, it grabbed my heart and pulled.

Tears welled, and I gave him a small, sad smile, which was stupid because I didn't have a right to be upset over something I knew all along wouldn't happen. I blamed the alcohol, though I suddenly felt very sober.

Country's gaze became intense as he studied me.

I needed out. I needed to leave before I said or did something I would regret.

From behind me, I heard Henri say, "I'm not doing it. He looks like he could kill me with his pinkie finger."

"For her. Get your ass up there and do it," Eve replied.

"Fine," Henri snapped.

Country nodded at something Wreck said, and then he took a step toward me. My heart hammered in my chest. I looked to my left, then right. I had to run. I had to get away from him.

But my feet were frozen.

My gaze kept straying back to Country as he approached like he was the light, and I was the bug transfixed by it.

Country stopped in front of me. I knew it because I saw his feet right *there*. His feet were big—which explained his dick size—and covered in boots. I'd always loved his boots. Then again, I enjoyed seeing anything he wore. But especially if he stood naked in front of me with all his tattoos on display.

"How you doin', Dusty?"

Nodding, with my gaze still on his feet, I threw in a shrug and a wave of the hand around in the air.

His chuckle sent a shiver over my body. "Why aren't you lookin' at me, darlin'?"

Because I'm afraid I'll jump you.

Because I'm scared I'll lick you.

Because I'm terrified you'll let me have another night with you, and my crush will grow while my heart breaks.

Yet, I couldn't say any of those things.

"Got something in my eyes," I mumbled.

"What'd you say, baby?"

Shut up, you good-looking piece of meat.

A throat cleared just before an arm slipped around my waist. "Thanks for keeping *my* woman company, but I got it from here. Can't leave such a fine ass alone for a moment before the dogs are hounding her."

I gaped up at Henri, since I'd never heard him use such a deep tone before, and he lifted a finger and tapped under the bottom of my jaw. I snapped my mouth closed.

"Who're you?" Country demanded.

"Her guy." Henri stared down at me, and his eyes widened for a second. "My love, let's go dance." His arm dropped from my shoulder, and he took my hand to lead me out onto the dance floor.

Once there, he pulled me close, guided my hips with his hands into a gentle sway, and ducked his head. To the outside, I expected it looked like a lover's caress on the neck or ear. In reality, Henri's excited voice filled my ear with "Oh my God, I nearly shit myself saying that. But it sounded cool, right? I mean, I totally sounded like a straight guy, right?"

Smiling, I nodded, resting my forehead to his shoulder. "You did, and I appreciate the save."

"I'm not sure I can do it again. I'm already in fear of my life. Did you see the glower on your guy? He looked ready to gut me right there and then."

Snorting, I lifted my head and shook it. "You're imagining it. He doesn't care if I'm with someone else."

Henri scoffed. "Are you blind? Along with gutting me, I was sure he was picturing cutting off my hand that was touching your waist."

Rolling my eyes, I shook my head again. "Nope. You're seeing things that aren't there because Country is a little scary."

"Scary? If I'm around the guy much longer, I'll need to wear a diaper. He's crazy handsome, but scary as well."

"I know." There was a little breathlessness in my voice. Damn it.

"I can't believe you've slept with him. I mean, I

would, but I might have a heart attack while we're at it."
Henri whimpered. "He's glaring this way. He's going to
kill me. Dusty, you're the only one I trust with my shop.
I'm giving it to you."

Laughing, I slapped his arm. "Quit it. He won't do
anything to you."

Henri didn't listen, though. "I'll be sad to die
without finding my one true partner in life, but it would
be worth it. I could even come one last time from having
his hands on me."

Snorting, I rolled my eyes at his dramatics. Over his
shoulder, I noticed Country wasn't even looking our
way. He was too busy speaking with State and Wreck.

He didn't care.

Why would he when he had so many women vying
for his attention?

"Mon amour, are you sure he doesn't want anything
from you?"

"Completely. The last time we slept together was
months ago. He hasn't come to me for more. He hasn't
even hinted at something. Not only that but he's taken
other women to bed since me. I'm just the poor
schmuck who allowed a part of her heart to cling to a
man who isn't my future." Sighing, I dropped my forehead to his shoulder, suddenly feeling more sober than I
wanted to. Henri gently ran his hand up and down my
back.

"I know the feeling of not being wanted, chèrie. I

know how hard it can be. Just know you have good friends who will help you through this."

I glanced up and patted his chest. "I know."

"It may be best to stay away from him as much as you can."

"I try," I groaned. "He just seems to turn up wherever I am."

Henri's brows dipped. "Then maybe—"

I covered his mouth with my hand. "Nope. Do not read into it. I did once, and it got me nowhere." With a sad smile and shrug, I added, "I'll get over him. Eventually."

"You will."

"I will."

"Definitely."

I nodded. "One day."

"Until then, enjoy your life and try to find someone else. I've found one-night stands help me fill the hole."

Smiling, I snorted. "I've already been thinking it, but it might be best to find someone outside of the club." Though, I'd have to leave the club to do so because of the rules. Club girls were only allowed to sleep with the brothers of the club. At the interview, it was explained the rule was mainly for safety. For both the brothers and the women.

"I agree, mon amour. I will help you find someone."

"No, you don't have to do that."

"Rest assured, I will venture out and find the perfect

man with a huge dong." Laughing, Henri spun me out and back into his arms. It was surprisingly good to talk all this out so it wasn't only in my head.

Time. It was all I needed.

Time without Country in it. For that to happen, I needed to dodge him in every way I could.

CHAPTER FIVE

Country

$\mathcal{A}$ nger as hot as fucking lava filled my veins as I watched Dusty and whoever the hell he was dancing. He had no goddamn right to touch her or make her smile or laugh. I needed to find everything I could about the asshole and then destroy him for thinking he could be a part of a club girl's life.

She belonged to the Diamond MC. Yet, when I saw her with Tech that night, I hadn't liked the easy flirty banter between them, which was why I'd stepped in and made sure Tech was busy enough that when he came back, the memory of them flirting together would have shifted. Thank fuck it had because I wasn't sure what I would have done.

A tight iron fist wrapped around my chest and

squeezed. Ever since the last time I'd tasted her, I couldn't get it out of my mind. She was always there, always filling up my space in little ways that kept me looking for her or wanting to seek her out.

"Prez, what's with the death look?" State asked at my side. His woman was back in the booth talking quietly to Eve.

"This is my normal look, fucker." The waitress appeared with a tray of drinks. I nodded toward the table, and she placed them there, turning back to me with a sultry smile. When I looked away, I heard her retreating footsteps.

Good. I wasn't in the mood.

"You still tellin' me it's normal when you'd usually have that woman under your arm in a second?"

"Not in the mood, State."

State snorted. "You're always in the mood."

Smirking, I asked, "You should pay more attention to your woman than me and my bedroom."

He chuckled. "My woman gets all the attention she needs, don't question that. But you ain't been yourself lately, and with me bein' second-in-command, I need to know if there's somethin' I should be worryin' about."

"It's nothin'."

"So not club business then. This about a woman? A certain woman who's on the dance floor with another man?"

"State," I warned before I slipped by and took a seat in the booth to swallow back my whiskey.

"Eve, it's none of our business. She'll kill us for saying anything." Courtney's tone was laced with panic.

"Someone needs to say something. For her own sanity."

"But not us. She's only opened up to us, and we can't throw that away by going behind her back about this."

Eve sighed. "I know, but... what could happen if he knew?"

Scrubbing a hand over my face, I bit back my groan and looked at the women. Both were eyeing me. "You got somethin' to say, say it." I could feel Lucas, West, and Adrik watching me, but I only paid attention to the women, since it was obvious they had something to say. Well, Eve did.

Courtney shook her head. "Nothing."

I quirked a brow. "Eve?"

"Don't," Courtney mumbled out the corner of her mouth. Did she not realize I could hear her, or did she just not give a fuck? Probably the second one, and I couldn't help but think again that State had picked well for his old lady.

Eve looked to the dance floor and back to me. "I have to."

"She'll kill you."

"Henri said—"

"Are you talkin' about that guy out there with Dusty? Who is he?"

Eve's gaze narrowed on me. "Why are you asking? Do you care who she's dancing with? Who she's been fucking? Who she's been kissing?"

The glass shattered in my hand at the thought of anyone kissing and fucking her. Glancing down at the glass and my bleeding hand, it finally fucking dawned on me why I couldn't keep Dusty off my mind.

She was mine.

Across the table, Lucas gasped. He was out of the booth quickly. "I'll get a first aid kit."

Eve cackled as Courtney looked at her like she'd grown a third eye. Eve waved her off and grinned at me. "I guess that answers that. Then you should know Dusty has a crush on you that she's trying to fight."

Even with the knowledge Dusty was into me, which had my dick thickening, annoyance over Dusty fighting what she was feeling had me grinding my teeth together, and I clipped, "Why would she fight it?"

Eve threw her head back and laughed. Courtney winced, and I glanced to see West shaking his head while Adrik snorted.

"What?" I demanded coldly.

"You're kidding, right?" Eve asked. When I said nothing and only stared, she sighed. "Country, have a think about what Dusty sees after you and her... bumped uglies."

"Just spit it out, Eve."

She straightened and lifted one finger. "Rochelle." Another finger joined the first. "Isla." Another. "Trissa." Another. "Davina, and that's only the few I know of."

Screwing my nose up, I bit out, "You been in my bedroom? You *know* I'm fuckin' all those pussies?"

Eve's head jerked back until she shook it and snapped, "Well, no. But they hang off you all the damn time, and you don't stop them."

"Watch your tone, woman. Not that I have to explain myself, but I fuckin' will. I don't stop them because I never thought Dusty would want more. As far as I knew, she only wanted me for my cock to get off. She didn't say anything. She didn't seek me out." I didn't always have eyes on her, so I couldn't be completely sure another brother hadn't been with her—fuck, that thought burned—but I presumed I wasn't the only one for her. It wasn't like the brothers and I talked about who we'd been with. For their safety, it was best I didn't know if Dusty had been with someone else. Turning a blind eye was better for my sanity.

But fuck, had I fucked up waiting on her?

Did we screw up by dancing around each other when we could have been it for one another? Knowing that was a possibility pissed me off to a point where I wanted to hit something or someone.

Maybe the fucker who had his hands still on Dusty.

But was what Dusty felt for me only something

small? Did she only want to fuck me and then nothing? I'd had many bitches like that, but I couldn't see Dusty being the same. She had a heart, and fuck me, it was big. She was always smiling, always willing to help, always sweet, funny, and damn smart.

"Who is that motherfucker with her?" I snarled.

"Henri. Her boss at the florist." Eve's answer had surprise flicking through me. "He's gay, and I was the one who asked him to act as a shield between you two because I knew Dusty was afraid of making a fool of herself in front of you."

What was Dusty afraid of saying? I wanted to know.

"I've gone against girl code here, and my friendship could be on the line, Country. She's the only club girl I like. Did I just fuck up, or do you want something more with Dusty?"

"None of your business, Eve."

"Country—"

"Enough. I like you, Eve, but never question me again."

I heard her sigh as I drew my gaze back out to the dance floor. My heart skipped a beat when I didn't see her anywhere. Quickly, I stood just as Lucas arrived. He tried to get me to sit back down, but I didn't listen, too busy glancing around for Dusty.

"Country, I got a text from Dusty." I turned to Courtney. "She's going home."

"The compound?"

"Well, no. To her own place."

When Lucas pressed his hand to my chest, I didn't resist and sat, letting him work on the small cuts.

Fuck me.

She left without knowing I'd grown a damn crush on her too. But my crush was different. My heart knew what it wanted, and it'd been Dusty for a while. It was why I hadn't been able to fuck the women she thought I'd been sleeping with.

Jesus Christ. It gutted me that Dusty had seen the women hanging off me and that I didn't put a stop to it when I should have. Made me damn sick to the stomach knowing she'd watched bitches with their hands on me when all I'd been wanting was her. But I'd been a fucking moron and touched those women back.

I wanted to shoot myself in the eye and bleach my hands and body. Thank fuck I could go to her and tell her I hadn't been inside any of them—not since the last time we'd been together. The thought of slipping into anyone but her brought bile to my throat. Hell, I'd only put up with Rochelle for a favor to her dad, an old friend. When I'd told him I'd keep her busy for the week —when he needed her attention elsewhere—he was grateful, as fucked-up as that sounded.

What did I do now that I knew Dusty was into me?

Did I go to her place and let her know I wanted her more than for just one night?

Did I wait her out?

If I did, it could take another few months, and that wasn't going to do for me. Not when I hungered for her like I had no woman before. But I also knew she was damn shy and nervous around me, so waiting might be the only option while I proved I was a born-again saint and didn't want another woman's attention.

"Ah, Country?" Courtney said at my side.

"Yeah?"

"With what Eve told you... Dusty's going to try and steer clear of you. She thinks she needs to get over her crush because you find her lacking, and then she added something you might not like because she's going to try and find someone else—" When my gaze snapped to her, she lifted her hands in front of her and gulped. "It was just what I caught her mumbling. Well, something along those lines anyway."

Like hell she'd find someone else.

"Lucas, move."

Wreck pulled his man out of the way as I stood. A hand gripped mine. "Country, listen. I'm a woman. I know what she'll need, and that's for you to prove you aren't interested in other women. If you rush to her now, she won't believe you. She'll think this'll be just for the night again, and there's a chance you could lose her altogether."

Prove to her she is it for me.

I could do that.

I would do that. Dusty deserved it and so much

more. I wished my heart had sorted out my head a while ago, then I would have had her in my arms that night. But it hadn't, so I'd deal with the consequences from not only hurting Dusty by my actions with other women but by making her see she was the only choice I saw in my future.

SMELLING SOMETHING GOOD TO EAT, I knew Dusty was in the kitchen. I'd only seen her a couple of times that week, and all were in passing. Now I had the chance to actually see her, and I felt like a fucking schoolboy with the way my gut was rolling.

On the way to the kitchen, brothers greeted me. Usually I'd stop for a chat, but I wasn't in the mood when I had someone else to see.

Slipping through the kitchen door, I spotted Dusty right away. She stood at the stove, stirring something. Tech had just stepped up to her with a plate and said something that made her laugh. I clenched my jaw. They'd been getting closer lately, which didn't sit well with me. I'd have to have a talk with Tech about it soon. Let him know Dusty was off-limits.

I grabbed a plate and was about to round the counter when an arm wound around my waist caught me by surprise. Glancing down, I bit back a curse when I saw Davina smiling up at me.

"Hey, Prez. It's good to see you."

Dusty's stirring stopped, and she stiffened. Yeah, she really didn't like the other women all over me. Again, my gut clenched that I'd hurt her in ways I didn't know. I wished I'd fucking manned up and done something about it, even when I wasn't sure if Dusty wanted more than a hookup from me.

"Davina." I nodded, putting down the plate. I grabbed her arms and gently pushed her back a step. I picked up the plate again and moved around the counter.

"Country," Davina cooed as she followed me. *Fuck.* "How about we do some catching up later?" Her hand slid up my back just as I reached Dusty's side. Tech smirked at me, probably thinking I'd be into Davina's attention, but it was the worst time for it.

"Davina, I'm busy. Go see another brother."

She giggled. "I'm sure I can change your mind." Her hand ran over my ass.

Turning to face her, I noted she took a step back from whatever she saw on my face. "When I say something, woman. I mean it. And don't touch me unless I fuckin' ask for it. Got it?"

Her face went bright red, and she glanced behind me to a silent Dusty. "Got it, Prez." She quickly walked from the room.

Tech also made his exit while I faced Dusty. I held my plate out and she took it.

"Having a tough morning?" she questioned softly, focusing on the pot. She hadn't looked at me yet, and I wanted her eyes.

"You could say that, darlin'." She handed me back the plate, and I took a step back to lean my ass against the counter as I grabbed a fork and started eating.

Dusty glanced over her shoulder, tensed, and looked back to the pot. Smiling, I took another mouthful. I liked knowing she was nervous with my proximity.

Moaning around a mouthful, I bumped my foot into the back of hers. "This is good, baby."

Redness coated her neck, and I grinned again. "Thanks?" It sounded more like a question than anything.

"You gonna have some?"

"I've already eaten." Her stomach growled at her obvious lie. Her blush deepened.

Chuckling, I stepped close with another plate. "You wouldn't be lyin' to me, Dusty?"

She snorted and flicked her gaze up to me, then back down to the pot and her constant stirring. "No... yes... I don't know why I did."

When she looked up as I shuffled closer, I winked and handed her the plate. "All good, darlin'. But I want to make sure you take care of yourself as well as others."

She licked her lips, and was that a small whimper? "Okay." She went to take the plate, but I held it out of her grasp and instead gently set her aside so I could dish her up some. Once done, I handed it to her and grabbed another clean fork set out on the counter, and held it out to her.

To my surprise, her hand shook a little when she took it. Yeah, she was nervous, but was something else going on inside her?

"Thank you," she mumbled. She started eating, looking everywhere but at me. I picked up my plate again and finished my food. The silence was comfortable for me, but I could see it was starting to get to Dusty. She'd opened and closed her mouth so many times, I was surprised she'd managed to eat still.

"Can I get you a drink?" I headed over to the refrigerator and opened it.

"Sure, just a bottle of water would be good. You know, ah, water is good for you."

Grinning into the fridge, I nodded. "Yeah, baby. I heard." I grabbed her bottle and myself a can of Coke. I placed both on the counter near her and reached out to swipe my thumb over the corner of her mouth. "Had some sauce there."

"Okay," she squeaked when I sucked the sauce off my thumb.

The doors to the kitchen opened, and Death walked in. "This a bad time? I can go, give you two time with your flirting."

Dusty snorted through her laugh. It was fucking cute. "No. He's... we're not flirting. I should... um..."

She placed her plate down and grabbed her water bottle "...go. Yeah. I need to go, not that I'm running from here, because I'm not, and there wasn't any flirting going on." She reached out with her free hand and punched my shoulder. "We're friends. Yeah, friends, and this friend"she thumbed at herself—"needs to get going." Her gaze dropped to the floor after frantically flicking from Death to me as she spoke. "Bye." She was out the doors before I could say anything.

Death watched her fly out of the room and then looked back to me, raising a brow. "You gonna claim her?"

"Yeah."

"About fuckin' time. I'm sick of watchin' you two eye fuck each other from across the room. Plus, you were screwin' shit up with her when you let those other bitches all over you."

"You could have told me to get my shit together ages ago."

Death smirked. "Where's the fun in that?" He sobered and headed over to the simmering pot. "She'll be good for you, Country."

"Know it now." And I couldn't fuckin' wait to make it happen. Still, I'd give her a little more time to get used to all my attention on her and no one else.

CHAPTER SIX

Dusty

hat was going on? I didn't know, but I worried there was a chance I was in a coma and dreaming up a Country who didn't pay attention to other women. In over a week, I hadn't seen him with a woman hanging off him.

"Maybe he's getting too old and can't get it up anymore." Davina laughed.

All right, I wasn't in a coma, and this was real, because there was no way I would let Davina in one of my fantasies.

The men were out on an evening ride, and the women were sitting around the dining room area talking, reading (which was me), or painting their fingernails as they gossiped. At Davina's words, anger lit me from within. No one talked shit about Country, or any brother, for that matter. Not when they had a cushy job by not doing much at all, and they got a room, food, and pleasure.

Some of the girls laughed. Strace caught my gaze and rolled her eyes.

"It wouldn't surprise me. I mean, he wasn't that good in bed last time," Amy said. She was another bitchy club girl like Davina.

Davina sighed. "His penis will be missed." Others laughed like the sheep they were while anger simmered under my skin at their talk. Even when they slept with members, they should keep it to themselves. I knew a lot of them wouldn't want the women spreading shit about them.

"I heard he could be taking steroids, so maybe his balls have shrunk and he's just not that horny anymore." Amy cackled like she'd said the funniest thing in the world

I flung my book at her head, knocking it sideways. "Bitch!" she cried. "He's not here to impress, Dusty, and why can't you get it through your thick head he's not interested?"

I didn't have to sit through this bullshit.

Slowly, I stood. "It's not about impressing anyone. It's about common courtesy. How dare you spread shit and talk about private things that the men, the brothers of the club who allow you to stay here, wouldn't want mentioned outside the bedroom. What gives you the right to talk shit? Just because you spread your legs for them? Your pussy isn't cased in gold. It isn't some magic portal taking you into a world where it's okay to talk about men in this club behind their backs." I honestly didn't know what I was rambling. I wasn't sure if I said things that either made sense or didn't, but at least they should get the gist of my meaning. If not, with my anger growing, I would knock it into their heads.

"Get off your high horse, Dusty. They probably do the same about us."

A laugh escaped me. "You honestly think the brothers of the Diamond MC would want to sit around swapping stories about who they fuck? They don't care who had you first or last. They want a night of stress-free lovemaking without the bitchiness attached." I threw out a hand. "Hell, you all live here for *free*. You don't even have to have a job outside of here if you don't want one. What you get from them is more than what you give. Show some decency and respect, and don't start spreading shit that you know is a *lie*."

My chest heaved with each breath as I looked around at all the women. Some seemed ashamed, some bored, but it was Davina and Amy who looked pissed.

Davina stood. "The girls have voted recently. We want you gone from here."

A fist grabbed my heart. I was that disliked they

wanted me gone? "What?" I breathed. Could they even do that?

I met Strace's gaze as she winced, but she quickly stood. "Not everyone voted you gone, Dusty. We see what you do around here."

Davina glared at Strace. "No woman should be able to stay unless they're putting out, and no one wants to go near her stinky ass."

They voted me out like some contest or something?

Me. The one who cooked, cleaned, and did so much more than any of them because I knew I was cheating the system by not sleeping with the brothers. But I couldn't sleep with anyone except for the one who had stolen my damn heart in the first place.

Even if they couldn't do this, maybe this was the sign I needed. Maybe it was best if I did leave and let these assholes step up to do the cooking, cleaning, and washing. I'd love to see them in a few weeks when they realized just what I did around here, and when none of it would be getting done, the brothers would notice, and they wouldn't like their women lazy.

Pulling back my shoulders, I smiled. "You know what. Fine. I'll go. Good luck with dealing with what I've been doing."

"Dusty, don't go." Strace started for me, but I shoved a hand up to stop her.

"Thanks for caring, Strace. But I don't need this shit.

I had enough bitches to deal with in high school. I don't have to deal with it here also."

Stalking off to my bedroom, I grabbed my suitcase from under my bed and had started loading my things into it when Strace came running in. "You're not really leaving, right?"

"I am." I was done. The only way I could come back was if Davina and Amy were gone. At least then the others might take more care about how they acted or what they said.

"Dusty, you can't just leave. You have to talk to Country and let him know. You know that."

"I'll talk to him." Eventually. Heck, it could be good to be away from the compound and Country, since he'd taken it upon himself to torture me with his eyes, his smiles, his winks. They'd been upped ten-fold compared to what he used to do, and I didn't know why.

Had he finally seen how good of an old lady I'd make?

"What are you laughing at?" Strace asked with a concerned look.

Waving a hand around, I shook my head. "Nothing. Just a joke in my head." I went into our bathroom and took my toothbrush and any other personal items I needed. Strace was leaning against the doorway, watching me. "Whatever I leave, you can keep. I really do appreciate that you've been kind."

"I could have been kinder, but I thought you didn't like me."

My head jerked back as the shock hit me. "Really?"

"You hardly speak to me, Dusty. Is it really that much of a shock?"

"I... ah... sorry?" I winced. "I know it's not an excuse, but I'm kind of an introvert, and I hated the thought of being a bother to anyone. I didn't reach out to anyone really until recently."

"I know." She smiled. "I've been here as long as you and noticed how shy you were. How it was only Country you wanted attention from. How you busied yourself with chores to make sure you're helpful in other areas. I'm not the only club girl who's noticed how much value you are to us and the club." She moved over to me and rested her hand on my upper arm. "You'll be missed."

My throat thickened and I sniffed. "Maybe we could catch up for a coffee outside of here?"

Her smile turned soft. "I'd like that."

Reaching out, I squeezed her hand. "Good. We'll definitely do it. You've got my number still?" I gave it to her a while ago to text me if she'd needed anything at the store.

"I do. Don't be a stranger, though." She bit her bottom lip. "I still think you should stay for Country to get back and talk to him."

My belly dropped at the idea. I didn't want him to

know I was so hated among the women that they voted me gone. Not that I was leaving for them. I had a feeling they'd soon ask me back, and I wanted them to beg.

Placing my toiletries in my suitcase, I zipped it up and headed to the door. With a quick hug and goodbye to Strace, I made my way out of the compound.

It wouldn't be too hard to stay with my parents. I was still there at least once a week to take care of the plants. Not that they knew.

This was for the best.

It was.

I had to believe that.

SINCE I ALREADY HAD PLENTY OF things at the house, I didn't bother dragging my suitcase out of the car and up all those stairs. Though, the noise would have been a reprieve from the silence that greeted me.

In my bedroom, I lay on my bed and sighed. Living here would take me an extra twenty minutes to Henri's florist and half an hour to the vet clinic. I picked up my phone beside me on the bed. I still had an hour before I had to leave, since the vet clinic stayed open late most nights and they wanted everyone gone before I could get in there to clean. Not that I minded. I had a lot of company from the pets staying there.

A door slammed closed downstairs, and voices

drifted up. I climbed off the bed, thinking it was better to see my parents than leave without saying anything at all.

Making my way downstairs, I walked into the kitchen, where they were talking about work. My parents owned a chain of hotels that were passed down from both their fathers before they joined together when Mom and Dad married. They were always busy overseeing them, which they seemed to enjoy, but I knew it wouldn't be for me. I preferred a simpler and happy life, even if that meant I worked more jobs I *enjoyed* than one I hated. It was better than being stressed all the time.

"Dusty, you're home." Dad smiled.

I returned it. "I am. How's things?"

Mom moved to the refrigerator. "Liam, do you want something to eat since we didn't get dinner? We've eaten all the meals the cook prepared for us, so it'll be something simple."

"I'd love something. I just have to make a quick call." He quickly walked from the room after a pat to my head.

Really, I should have been used to this, but I still tensed up. At least Dad had acknowledged me.

Pushing my feelings back, I moved over to the counter. "Do you need some help, Mom?"

"Hmm?" She grabbed things out and then a pan.

"Do you need help?" I tried again.

Her phone chimed with a message, and she picked it

up. "Dusty, can you put some omelets together while I get back to this?" She waved her phone around, then stared at the screen, clicking things.

Moving around the counter, I got to making them dinner, glancing at Mom as she typed away. "I had a sex change while I was gone."

"That's nice, sweetie."

Tears welled. "Yep, I have a nice big dong now."

"Good, good."

Unclenching my jaw, I bit out, "I even got it pierced."

"Uh-huh."

"Then I got gangbanged by four huge bikers."

"Okay."

Sighing, I put the knife down and walked out of the room. She didn't even know I'd gone. At the bottom of the stairs, I saw Dad come out of his office. He smiled, but it faded when he took me in.

"Dusty, are you all right?"

It was the first time he'd asked me in a long time. Yet, I couldn't bring myself to say what was wrong—how I was fed up with being ignored or put last all the time. I was tired of it. They had cleaners and many people working under them who they could order around. They didn't care what I did as long as I didn't get in the way.

"I'm fine. Did you need something?"

He squinted. "Did we miss your birthday? I can run out now and get a happy nineteenth birthday card."

Nineteenth. God, I wanted to laugh in his face.

Shaking my head, I started up the stairs. "I was nineteen two years ago, Dad."

"Dusty—"

"I have to get to work."

"Work? This late? Where? I thought you were going into that horticulture degree to work as a florist."

"I didn't, but I am working as a florist. I have another job as well. Which I've got to get to. Bye," I said calmly, even when I wanted to bash his head into the wall. But they weren't completely to blame. I could have tried harder to get their attention. I didn't because the few times I had, I hated their annoyed expressions.

Which was why it was easier to live away from them. They had their lives. I had mine to live however I wanted to. Though, until—or if—I went back into the Diamond MC, I'd stay here... no matter how much it depressed me.

Quickly, I left and drove to the veterinary clinic. I couldn't wait to get to work, even as I yawned, because my mood always lifted around the animals.

Pulling into the parking lot out front, I switched off the engine and climbed out, swinging my bag over my shoulder. With my keys in my hand, I found the one for the front door to the clinic and quickly walked there. The gravel crunched under my feet with my quick pace. I disliked the area. Until I was locked inside, I wouldn't relax. There were only a few other shops in the area, but all were closed at this time of the day. Plus, on the other side of the road, there was nothing but open space that was waiting to be developed into a home estate. I took a quick glance behind me as I reached the door and noticed a car parked down the road a little with its headlights off. I could make out two people sitting inside it from the lamppost just opposite.

Why would they be sitting in a car this late at night and this area?

It didn't make sense, and honestly, it freaked me out. My hands shook when I unlocked the door and took one last glance at the car. My heart jumped into my throat when it started, and the headlights shone. I stepped through the door and closed it, flicking the lock into place and shutting off the alarm system.

Moving to the side, I peered back out the window and shivered as the car drove by slowly. I couldn't be positive, but I had a feeling they were looking toward the clinic. I'd have to make sure to let the owner know, since they'd previously been broken into. Only it had been before I started working there.

Sighing, I checked the lock again and reengaged the alarm. When the car was out of sight, I stayed at the window for a while longer to make sure it didn't return. There was no way someone could get in the back of the clinic because that was where the dogs who stayed overnight were, and they would make enough noise to scare anyone off. I hoped.

Rubbing a hand over the back of my neck, I walked to the counter and then behind it to store my handbag. All the cleaning supplies were provided, so I made my way to the cupboard for them. I had to do the dusting, vacuuming, mopping, and wiping down benches, seats, window blinds, and tables in the waiting area. It usually took me a few hours, but I was always late getting out because my reward was to see the animals at the end, and it was always hard to leave them.

The only problem with cleaning was that the music I listened to wasn't enough to distract my mind. I knew I had to ring Country, but I wondered if putting it off would be okay. My blood pumped faster at the thought of him. There was a chance he wouldn't notice I wasn't around for a few days. Okay, there was a possibility the brothers would miss my cooking, but I was sure Courtney would organize something with the other girls. She'd taken on the mother hen role when she and State had been together for a while. Though, she hadn't needed to run much since I'd been around and doing most of it.

Maybe I needed to call her as well to give her a heads-up. I still wasn't sure I made the right choice, but the thought of proving to those bitches I was needed at the compound appealed to me more. Though, would I be strong enough to stay away from the only place I felt was home? Time would tell.

CHAPTER SEVEN

Country

We'd been back at the compound for an hour, and I still hadn't seen Dusty. She wasn't here when we'd walked in the dining area, and all the club girls were mingling about, shooting the shit. They quickly packed up their woman stuff and plastered themselves to whichever brother was in the mood for them.

Davina and Amy tried to get my attention, but I wasn't having it. Soon they'd know why—when I claimed Dusty in a way everyone understood she was mine.

I was sitting at a table with Tech and Quake. Neither of them had a girl hanging off them, and a bitter taste filled my mouth at the thought of them waiting for Dusty to appear like I was.

It was time to have a chat.

"Brothers." When I had their attention, I swallowed a sip of beer and placed it on the table. "Gonna grow somethin' between Dusty and me. Need to know you two don't have anythin' for her, and if you do, you need to back the fuck off because I ain't willin' to share or give her up."

Quake grinned. "Think it's cool, Prez. I didn't miss the way she acted around you. I know I was placed in the friend zone right from the start."

Nodding, I turned to Tech. He was more unknown because I knew he'd been into her and would have slept with her if they had a chance. I just made sure they didn't.

Tech chuckled. "Got nothin' to worry about with me, Prez. She'll be good for you."

"Know that."

"When you gonna make it clear to everyone?" Tech asked before gulping back his beer.

"When she agrees with me that we have somethin' to work on."

"Good luck, brother." Quake saluted me with his beer before taking a pull.

Tech snorted. "Yeah, you might need it. She can be a spitfire."

Quake shook his head. "She still gets too flustered

around the prez to get pissed. Just don't play *Halo* with her, and she'll let you keep your balls."

Tech guffawed. "Does that mean she'd got yours?"

A growled "Better fuckin' not" had Quake quickly shaking his head.

"Nope, fuck no. Only balls she's ever wanted are Prez's."

"Can we goddamn quit talkin' about balls?" I clipped.

"Is it creepin' you out, Prez? What happens if Dusty wants to talk about balls? Are you willin' to ball talk with her? Is she that kinda special?" Tech, the fucker, was close to getting a black eye.

Quake's face morphed into something I hadn't seen, but I could work out he was trying to hold back his laughter. Damn assholes.

Sighing, I scrubbed a hand over my face before I stood. "Think yourself lucky I have to get to fuckin' work. Get word out if anyone needs me, I'll be at Polished."

Tech grinned. "You got it. I'm gonna go find Dusty, see if she wants to talk about balls—" Tech fell off his seat when I went to grab for him. He shot to his feet, hands out, laughing, "Fuck, I'm kiddin', I'm kiddin'."

Shooting him the middle finger, I stalked out of there and went to my ride. I'd only had one drink, so I was all right to ride again. Fucking sucked I didn't get a chance to see Dusty, but if she was hiding in her room, I'd give her that and seek her out tomorrow.

A grin tugged at my lips. I could even make tomorrow the day I'd have a chat with her about what I wanted and see if she was on the same page. I had a feeling she would be, but I didn't know if I'd given her enough time for her to trust that I didn't want anyone else's attention but hers.

The ride to Polished was quick when I had my woman on my mind. It was good to see the parking lot full when I pulled into my reserved spot. Business was booming. I was damn glad State, Saint, and I went into this together. It was bringing in enough cash that we were sitting pretty. Most of the time the job was easy. It was when a fuckwad got rough with the girls or guys that we'd step in. The downside was bookwork.

Up in my office that I shared with State, I opened the door and found him sitting behind the desk. He stood as soon as I entered.

"That time already?"

"Sure is. Lookin' busy."

"Hell yeah. We might even need to hire a few more girls with the way things are goin'. Plus, we still need to replace West and Gun. I've left some résumés on the desk. Made a note of which ones I reckon could work. See what you think."

"Will do."

"Wanna know somethin' interestin'?"

"What?"

"Dusty hasn't been with another brother."

My blood froze in my veins. "Say again?"

State smirked. "None of them but you."

"How the fuck do you know this?" And why did the news shoot adrenaline to my pulse and cock?

"Been askin' around. It ain't like the brothers weren't interested, but they never pushed her 'cause they noted her attention seemed to be on you."

Holy fucking shit. She'd always been mine. Christ, I felt like a dickhead for not seeing it.

"Anyway, I better get home. Crispin's been sleepin' shit lately with more of his teeth comin' in. Court will need a break, no doubt."

Never thought I'd see State settled with a woman, but he knew Courtney was his from the first night. Hell, why couldn't I have been smart with Dusty in the first place as well?

Soon things would change.

Very fucking soon.

DRAGGING my feet since I was goddamn tired, I made my way into the compound the next day. I needed a shower, sleep, coffee, and to see my woman, in that order. Hell, I could even use a sighting of Dusty before any of the other things.

It was around lunchtime, but I couldn't smell anything cooking. Not that she did it every day. I didn't bother heading to the kitchen; instead, I went past her room. The room was open, but she wasn't in there. Christ, it was probably for the best. There was a chance that, in my tired state, I'd probably ask her to marry me or some shit.

I ended up crashing for a good five hours, which took me to dinnertime. I got dressed and headed down for coffee. The dining room was scattered with people, and before I could reach the kitchen, a club girl stepped in front of me.

Stracy.

"Country—"

'Not interested, babe. Hit up a brother." I went to move around her, but she grabbed my arm.

"No, it's not that. It's about Dusty. I just wanted to check she called you."

Facing her, I crossed my arms over my chest. "Called me about what?"

She flushed and tugged at her mini shorts. "I-I...." She sucked in a breath. "You looked too calm. It's why I didn't think you knew."

Annoyance hardened my tone. "Knew about what, woman?"

Davina appeared next to her and threaded her arm through Stracy's, who stiffened. "Hey, handsome, are you busy right now?"

"Get lost, Davina," I clipped.

"Sure, sure. I just need to speak with—"

"Now," I snarled, glowering down at her. Davina pissed off, but I didn't miss the pinch she placed on Stracy's arm. Meeting her gaze, I nodded toward the hall. "Let's talk in my office." Stracy nodded, and along the way, I called, "Death, Tech. Office." They both stood and followed instantly. I didn't know the situation, but in case I needed backup, it was good to have brothers close.

Opening my office door, I walked in and around the desk to sit behind it. "Sit." I lifted my chin toward a chair for Stracy to take. Tech and Death moved into the room. Death took a spot on the right side, resting back against a file cabinet. Tech, after closing the door, stood by it.

Leaning forward, I steepled my hands and eyed Stracy. "Now, wanna tell me why you think Dusty would call me?"

She shifted on the seat, cleared her throat, and swallowed nervously. "There was a situation yesterday with the women—"

A knock sounded. Tech opened the door, and I heard two voices, one a woman's, the other a man's. Tech turned to me. "State and Courtney. Sounds like it's about the situation Stracy's talkin' about."

Nodding, I waved a hand, and Tech opened the door further. Both stepped in before he closed it again. The room was crowded, but I didn't care. I needed to get to the bottom of it.

Courtney placed her hands on her hips. "I got a text from Dusty earlier, and do you know what it said?" She took a breath and went on. "It said that I might need to dole out jobs to the girls here because *Dusty* was voted out by them."

My gaze snapped to Stracy. "What the fuck happened?" I thundered.

Stracy flinched, but she pushed her shoulders back and told me, "Dusty has never been a favorite with the girls because she doesn't sleep with any of the guys. Yesterday, a couple of them were saying stuff that Dusty didn't like. She went off on them, and Davina told her about the girls voting and said she should go because no one liked her. I tried to let Dusty know it wasn't all the girls' opinions, but she wouldn't listen."

"Where did this happen?" Tech asked while my body burned with anger. Those fucking stupid cunts were nothing without Dusty around. They didn't do anything like she did. I never missed the way Dusty stepped up and took care of this place and us.

Stracy licked her dry lips. "The dining area."

"Tech?" I bit out.

"Yeah, it'll be on video."

"Go to your workroom and get it up. I'll be there in a moment." Tech quickly left. I leaned back to grab a piece of paper and looked back to Stracy. "I want to know who voted Dusty out. All the names. Then you need to tell me who you think only voted because of pressure."

When she nodded, I slid the paper her way with a pen, and she got to work.

Glancing up to Courtney, I told her, "Do you have time to delegate tasks around here?"

"Yeah. I only stopped since Dusty seemed happy to do what she was."

Grunting, I tipped my chin to the door. "State, go with your woman. Court, can you do it now, and I want both of you to take note of who complains."

Courtney saluted me. "You got it, captain."

State snorted, curled an arm around his woman, and led her out. Standing, I ordered, "Death, see Stracy to her room to finish that list and then meet me in Tech's lab."

"You got it, Prez. Come on, babe." As soon as they were gone, I locked up my office and headed down to the end of the hall where Tech was situated in his computer room. Entering, I watched his fingers fly across the keys before I looked up to the seventy-inch screen on the wall. A video was paused. It showed the full dining area and the group of women sitting around. I noticed Dusty sat farther away with a book in her hand.

"What we got, brother?" I stepped up to his side.

"If you hadn't already claimed her, I would have after seeing this video."

"Do not even fuckin' mess around sayin' shit like that."

"It's cool, Prez. I know she's yours. But seriously, wait until you see this shit. Bitches can be fuckin' assholes." He glanced behind him. "We waitin' on anyone else?"

"Death. He's taken Stracy to her room to write out who voted Dusty out."

"You know Davina's got to go, right? She might look pretty, but the cat has claws, and she's been huntin' for a piece of you for a long time."

"I might have been a fuckin' fool by givin' her attention, but she's never had a piece of me, and she never will. I know a manipulative bitch when I see one. I'd hoped she'd grown out of it since Hooch seems to like her pussy, but she likes messin' with others too much to see she could have had a good thing with a brother if she'd kept her claws away from Dusty."

"She's power-hungry too. Before you got here, I had a quick look at some other videos starring her, and it's clear she'd been wantin' to be the one in charge of all the club girls and who they get to sleep with."

"Fuckin' hell. Why do we even bother with bitches?"

"Because the brothers like an easy lay. We did also."

Groaning, I scrubbed a hand over my face. "Christ."

"Even though I don't fuck 'em," Death started as he walked into the room, "it doesn't go by me they seem better when Davi isn't around. Make the bad seed go, and things'll get better."

"Let's see if there's more than one bad seed, though." I nodded to the screen, and Tech hit Play. The first words had me clenching my hands at my side and grinding my teeth together. The vile cunts were spreading shit about me. My eyes widened when Dusty threw a book at one of the bitches' heads. She stood, and the words out of her mouth had me gaping like a lovesick fool with a hard-on for the first time.

"Jesus," I muttered. Now I understood why Tech said what he did. She was fucking perfect. Having our backs without another thought, and she did it goddamn beautifully.

"Marry the fuck outta her," Death said with a slap to my back.

"Plannin' to." I knew we were compatible in bed, and I liked what I saw in how she acted.

Christ, I couldn't wait until she was mine.

"That was inspirational shit." Tech clicked Stop on the video.

"Davina and Amy are gone. Death, go grab Stracy's list. I want to see who else is outta here. Let it be known I'm callin' a meetin' with everyone in the dining room in half an hour."

"On it." Death nodded and left.

"Is there anythin' else pressin' I need to know about Davina?"

Tech shook his head. "Told you about the rest, but the shit you've seen is already enough to kick the ho out. Want me to make a voice recording of what was said to play in front of the brothers? Know they say shit about you, but if you're staking claim to Dusty, it won't matter."

"Do it." I didn't give a shit who heard what they said; the brothers wouldn't believe some slut anyway. "I'm gonna make a call. Meet you in the dining room."

Tech grinned. "You got it, and say hi to Dusty for me."

"No." I went back to my office for some quiet and pulled up Dusty's number. At the time of saving it, I was sure I'd never use it, since she was the only club girl's number saved in my phone.

"Dusty's phone, Henri speaking."

Henri. The gay guy who pretended to be Dusty's man. Even though I knew he was gay, I wanted to reach through the phone and strangle him because he got to dance with her. He got to touch her.

"Hello?"

"Is Dusty there?"

"Who is this? Wait, I didn't look at the caller ID when I answered…. Oh."

Oh was right.

His tone changed, became deeper. "Dusty's not here right now, and she accidentally left her phone at the shop—I mean at my place."

Sighing, I pinched the bridge of my nose. "I know who you are, Henri."

"You do?" he squeaked.

"You're her boss. Do you know where she is?"

"Is there a reason you're calling? I mean, I know who you are as well, and I don't think Dusty needs to hear from you unless you're ringing to confess your undying love for her. If that's not the case, then I think I need to delete this call, and when she comes for her phone, I'll pretend I haven't heard from you."

I liked he wanted to protect her, but it also gripped my gut in annoyance.

"Henri—"

"I know you can kill me and hide my body, though it would be a waste to the gay community, but Dusty is important to me, and I am to her, so please don't kill me."

"I'm not gonna fuckin' kill you," I clipped. "When you see Dusty, get her to call me. It's important." When he didn't reply, I growled, "You don't have to worry about her gettin' hurt by me."

"Well, all right then. As soon as her pretty face appears, I'll have her call you. Au revoir." He hung up, and I knew there was still the possibility I would strangle him for just getting on my nerves.

Pocketing my phone, I made my way out into the dining room. People sat or stood around, and when I caught Davina's gaze, she smiled and winked.

Ignoring it, I walked up to Death, who handed me the paper. I ran my gaze over it before nodding and handing it back. I went over and stood outside the kitchen doors and crossed my arms over my chest. The room quieted.

"Things are about to change. As soon as you've heard this, you'll understand why." I nodded to Tech, and the women's voices filled the speakers. No one laughed at what the women were saying. Instead, the brothers turned to glare at Davina and Amy.

I caught Death's and State's gaze, nodding toward the exits. They slipped through the crowd and collected a couple of brothers on the way to block the exits in case someone wanted to leave before I got to have a word with them.

Davina and Amy paled. Amy backed up until a brother pushed her forward, and she let out a cry, dropping to her knees. Davina just stood there as people moved away from her.

Brothers hooted and cheered at Dusty's words, and when the video stopped, they stomped their feet, calling Dusty's name.

"Tell me you're gettin' Dusty back, Prez" was called out when things settled.

Raising my hand, the room quieted again. "Davina, Amy, Riley, and Megan. You're no longer club girls. You leave here today knowin' that no one in the Diamond MC will touch you ever again. You leave knowin' that if you cause any trouble to us and ours, you will be dealt with in the worst kinda way."

"Wait." Eve strode forward and stepped in front of Davina. She cocked her fist back and punched her in the face. Davina's head rocked back, and she covered her nose with both hands. Eve, being slightly taller than Davina, gripped the top of Davina's hair and pulled her close. "Dusty is one hundred times better as a person and woman than you'll ever be. Come at her again in any goddamn way, I'll cut your throat." She shoved her back, and Davina fell to her ass. Tech rolled his eyes at his sister, but I was fucking grateful for her actions, since I didn't hit women. I was legit worried about Dusty, so Davina deserved it.

"Up, get your shit, and get out," I bit out. When they didn't move fast enough, I roared, "Now." They scrambled into action. Saint, Torch, Quake, Gun, and Death made sure to follow the women, to watch them grab their things and nothing else. Then they'd shadow them out of the compound.

"What about Dusty?" someone from the back called.

"I'll get to that shortly." It didn't take long for the women to come back down the stairs and the curses to rise from the men as they were marched out. When the brothers were back, I cleared my throat and people became silent. "Regardin' Dusty. The way she had our backs proved she's family. Though, she'll be more than that. Need you to know, brothers, that I'm gonna see if Dusty'll take me on as her old man."

Cheers and hooting roared around the room, and I couldn't help but smile. Yeah, Dusty would make the perfect old lady for the president. Now I just had to make sure she'd agree with me.

CHAPTER EIGHT

Dusty

It wasn't until I arrived home and went to reach for my phone to check the time that I realized I'd left it at the florist. Silently cursing myself, I decided it could wait until tomorrow. I had yard work to do before dinner and then cleaning at the clinic.

Tonight wasn't my usual evening to clean, but it was needed because of a few messy situations, apparently. I'd spoken to the owner about the car I saw the previous night. He'd been thinking of getting outside cameras anyway, but it would be moved up on the schedule. Then he asked if I wanted someone present tonight to keep me company. He was an older, caring man, but I reassured him I would be fine. I doubted whoever it was would come back, since they knew I'd seen them the night before.

After changing into yard clothes, I made my way back outside and into the shed for supplies. Usually, I did my work with music, but having forgotten my phone, I couldn't. It was how I heard a car pull up to the house.

My parents weren't home, so I had to check. It could be one of the cleaners, or the part-time cook Mom hired just yesterday. Walking around the front, I didn't catch anyone, but I heard the front door close before I could see who it was.

To be sure it was someone who was supposed to be there, I walked up the stairs to the front door and entered. Voices, two female ones, came from the living room to the left. One that was hardly used and mainly for business guests.

As I got closer, the voices became more prominent, and I knew one was Mom. "I don't doubt your choice, Charlie, but I wish you had told me before you left her."

"Why? Isn't this what we've been talking about? Change?" Charlie, the other woman, said.

"I am tired. Nothing in this house appeals to me."

I wasn't sure of the content of the conversation, but I wondered if Mom was thinking of selling. But then why would she want to know...? Instead of guessing, I opened the door and froze.

Both women broke from the passionate kiss to stare at me.

Mom sighed and removed her hands from… Charlie, whoever she was. "Dusty, I didn't think you'd be home. You hardly are these days."

Licking my dry lips, I shook my head. "Actually, these last couple of days, I'm home more than I have been." *You just didn't notice or care where I was or with whom.* "Does Dad know about this?"

Mom laughed. "Of course he does."

Right. I just didn't know. I got it loud and clear; it was none of my business.

"Well, if you'll excuse me, I'll get back to the yard."

"Rebecca," I heard from Charlie as I turned.

"Dusty, wait." Mom sighed again. I faced them, and Mom blindly reached for Charlie's hand, who took it instantly. My eyes widened a little at Mom's display of affection, even small as it was, because I'd never seen Mom and Dad share a kiss or embrace or even hold hands. "Charlie, I'd like you to meet Dusty. Dusty, this is Charlie. We're… we are dating." Her brows pinched together, and I wondered if she feared what I thought of my mom with another woman. She wouldn't know it didn't bother me, especially as I believed her when she'd said Dad knew. They'd never really been in love. It was always about business over anything. If this was who Mom could be happy with, then it was fine by me.

"It's nice to meet you, Charlie." Turning again, I stopped when Mom called my name.

When she had my eyes, she said, "Eventually, I'll be moving out and living with Charlie, and your father will move in with his partner."

What did she want me to say? I was shocked to know Dad had someone also, but again, I didn't care. It was obviously clear I knew nothing about my parents. When I'd tried getting to know them when I was younger, they changed the subject, and I was pushed aside for their work.

The sooner I could get out of here, the better. Maybe I could ask Henri if I could stay with him until I either pulled my thumb out and found my own place or went back to the Diamond MC.

Shrugging, I replied, "Okay. I shouldn't be here for too much longer. If I'm in the way now, I'll leave sooner."

Charlie gaped and looked to my mom, then back to me. When Mom said nothing else, I nodded and walked out, closing the door after me.

"Rebecca, what on earth was that? You and your daughter seem like strangers."

I paused, wanting to know how Mom would reply. "We are, and I believe it's all my fault. I built a wall around me because she's not mine."

My heart stilled its beating; my breath caught in my throat.

"Does she know?"

"No. Liam begged me to be the mother I could be when her mother, his ex, passed away after giving birth to her."

"What in the world?"

My thoughts exactly. I couldn't stay and listen. I staggered back outside and gripped at my tee over my belly, which twisted at the news my mother wasn't my real mom.

A laugh bubbled up and out. It made sense. Dad had always been the softer one when I was younger. Yet, he still held me at arm's length. Why? Did I remind him of my dead mother, or did he just not care?

Tears welled, and I drew in a shuddering breath. My head was about to explode with all the thoughts running through it. I couldn't take it. I couldn't pinpoint which question was more important, but I was also afraid if I asked either of them anything, they wouldn't tell me and brush it all aside.

Groaning, I wiped at my eyes. Did I really want answers? Would they get me anywhere? Nothing would change. They'd still put work and their "other" lives ahead of me.

Laughing humorlessly again, I went back to the yard and threw myself into work, hoping it would take my mind off all I'd discovered.

Hours later, as I drove to work, the new knowledge still played on my mind. Did I leave it alone and forget about it or find out who my mother really was and see if I had other family? Why would they hold this information from me in the first place? Honestly, they were probably too lazy to give me the time to share this news and then have *me* ask many questions. It wouldn't surprise me.

What I needed to do was get my work done, sleep, and wake up to a new day, which would hopefully provide me with the best way to go about the situation.

Turning on the street, I heard a loud pop before the back of my car dropped down a little. I gripped the wheel hard. "Shit," I muttered, pulling to the side of the road outside a factory not far from the clinic. Switching off the car, I climbed out and right away saw the problem. My back left tire had blown. From what, I didn't know. Sighing, I looked to the sky and cursed some more, remembering I hadn't replaced the spare.

"What the hell am I supposed to do?" Stomping back to the driver's door, I leaned in and grabbed my bag and keys. I locked the car and glared at it before I started walking to work.

"Yeah, Dusty, this is really smart. Work late at night, not replace your spare tire, forget your phone. Jesus." I glanced around and shivered. The factory was the only place open, but the further I walked away from it, the quieter it became. Luckily there were no creepy cars lingering on the side of the road. Though I was a bit earlier than last time, since I wanted to get away from the house in case Dad got home and Mom had spoken to him about me meeting Charlie.

Once inside the clinic with the alarm rearmed, I screwed up my nose at the scent. There had definitely been a few pet accidents. Even the waiting room still stank. I quickly got to work, only to pout when I realized I was going to have to deal without music again. I had just finished vacuuming and was placing it back in the storage closet when I froze at the sound of voices outside. Silently, I made my way down the hall to peek around the corner to the front windows and door.

"Come on, Brian. I thought you knew this shit." A man stood beside the door and kept glancing around.

"I do, dickhead. Just give me a damn moment," another man, Brian, said from his crouched position at the door.

Shit, fuck, shit. I pressed my back to the wall and gripped my top. My heart beat so fast it had my ears ringing. *What do I do? What do I do?* Why were they even breaking in? Didn't they see the lights on? Didn't they know someone was here?

But my car wasn't out front.

Fucking hell.

I... I have to do something.

If I snuck out the back, the dogs would warn them of my presence when they barked. They could follow me and catch me. *Fuck. What do I do?* If I stayed where I was, they'd soon find me. I needed a fucking phone. My stomach twisted as blood rushed to my head. I needed a phone. Which phone? I took one quick look back around to see that Brian guy was still working the lock on the door. Did they know about the alarm? Maybe if I stayed hidden, the alarm would go off, and the security company would send someone to check it out.

Carefully, I shot down the other end of the hall to one of the consultation rooms. My hands shook as I slowly opened the door and closed it behind me. The light was already on. I always lit up the rooms when I was cleaning. Did I turn it off to hide?

I didn't know.

I. Didn't. Know.

My breaths came out in short pants. I walked to the other door that led out into the room where the medicine was kept but then thought against it just as my eyes snagged on the phone.

With a gasp, I picked up the cordless phone, glanced around, and moved to the desk where the computer was. I got into the corner, as close to the desk as I could to hide. I fumbled the number a couple of times until I got it right and put it to my ear.

In the silence around me, I heard footsteps, doors opening, and then bickering in the medicine room. I covered my mouth.

"Who's this?" Country answered.

Fuck. Why did I call him? Why didn't I call the cops? *Stupid, stupid, stupid.*

"Country," I whispered. It was too late to call the cops, and I feared if I hung up, Country would call back and they'd find me. For now, they were busy stealing drugs.

Please, Country. Please, help me.

Country

"DUSTY?" I muttered, brows dropping low in confusion. Why was she whispering? Why did she sound scared? Quickly, I stood from the table in the dining room at the compound and clicked my fingers. I pointed at Tech and Death. "Baby, are you okay?"

I pressed the phone closer to my ear as I strode down the hallway to my office. I needed quiet. The hairs on my arms and the back of my neck rose at the thought of something going on with Dusty.

"Two men broke into the vet clinic. I-I was supposed to call the police, but…"

She'd called me instead. In her fear.

Stalking back out of the office, I nearly bumped into Death and Tech. "It's all right, darlin'. We'll come. Where are you in the clinic?" Once in the dining room, I covered the phone and whistled before I kept rushing to the exit. I already knew where the clinic was, and I cursed silently at the distance. But the cops were even farther, and I didn't trust they'd deal with whoever these fuckers were like we could.

"End of the hall office."

"Okay, baby. We're comin'." Once outside, I ordered, "Take the car." Death nodded and caught the keys I threw at him. "Darlin', stay on the phone with me, yeah?"

"Okay." Her soft, fear-filled voice gripped my heart. I climbed in the passenger seat, Death behind the wheel and Tech in the back. Brothers were following on their rides. They didn't know what was going on but came because they knew their president needed them.

Dusty whimpered.

"Baby?"

"T-They're close," she muttered.

Fuck.

"We're on our way, darlin'." My throat thickened at the thought of them finding her. "Fuck, if… if they come in, baby, I need you to tell me what they look like. Anything you can. Then you hand the phone over if they demand it. Yeah?" She hummed under her breath. My knee bounced up and down in agitation. I wanted to be there already. "Stay hidden, Dusty."

Death drove like a damn maniac, and I was grateful for it. But I couldn't stop the terror ripping through me at the thought of them finding her. Closing my eyes, I listened to everything as I rested my head back. I could hear her breathing, heavy, full of distress, but also in the background, things were being thrown around.

Don't find her, don't find her. Please.

I straightened when I heard a bang. I wanted to call out to Dusty, have her reassure me, but then her voice rang through the phone. "Dreads long, dirty, pale—"

"What the fuck?" was yelled.

"Skull tattoo on neck, short, hair dark—" Dusty let out a cry.

"Who the fuck you talking to, bitch?"

"One named Brian," I heard Dusty shout before she cried out. My heart crept up to the throat, and I gripped my cell tighter.

"Hang up the phone. It could be the cops. We got to get out of here."

"Who's this?" a voice I wouldn't misplace spoke into the phone. Cursing sounded in the background.

"Country, president to the Diamond MC. You touch the woman in front of you, we'll hunt and kill you. Leave now with whatever you have, and we'll let this drop."

The fucker laughed. "Yeah, right. You'll come after us no matter."

A rock formed in my gut. "I won't. You have my goddamn word. Leave the woman and go."

Dusty screamed just as the line disconnected.

"Fuck!" I roared.

"What they say?" Death asked.

"He didn't believe me." He didn't fucking believe me, but they'd better listen. "Get us there, Death." He pushed his foot harder to the pedal, but the rock of dread in my gut was growing. Even more so by the time we arrived fifteen minutes later. I was out of the car before Death had it in Park and running for the open door.

"Dusty?" I called, striding down the hall. "Dusty?" I yelled.

Nothing but silence greeted me. Then my brothers were there as I entered the last room. There'd been a struggle. My woman had fought.

"Search the area now for Dusty. Fucking find her."

Find her and bring her back to me. If not, I was going to lose my shit, and that wouldn't be good. I'd make anyone bleed to get her back.

CHAPTER NINE

Country

Quake stayed back at the clinic to speak to the police. I had him call them when we'd found all the information we could from there. We'd guessed that the cunts who'd taken Dusty hadn't known she was on site, since her car had been down the road with a flat tire. Quake's excuse for being there was that before Dusty disappeared, she had called us to fix her car.

The cops would do their own investigation, and if they found out shit before us, we'd keep tabs on them for any information they got. We needed to be sure we reached Dusty first. We had to be the ones to deal out justice.

"Anythin'?" I asked Tech for the tenth time.

"Not yet. Other than Quake being taken in for questioning." His fingers didn't stop flying over the keyboard, even when I picked up a chair and threw it against the wall with a roar.

I hated waiting.

I hated not knowing.

"We'll find her," State said from the doorway where he leaned. Death grunted, agreeing with State's statement.

We would.

We had to.

Gripping my hair, I dropped my head back and ran the call repeatedly in my mind. I'd already told Tech everything, but maybe there was something I'd missed.

Straightening, I rubbed at my chest and ordered, "Call Adrik. Get his men onto lookin'." I needed everyone we knew searching, digging up any information they could on the minimal information we had.

"I'll get Torch to call." State disappeared from the doorway.

Turning to Death, I rested my hands on my hips. "Shut Polished down. I want all brothers who work there on the streets, talkin' to everyone they know with the description we have. Someone has to fuckin' know them."

Death nodded and lifted his phone to his ear. "Saint, situation, shut Polished down and send the brothers to the streets. Dusty's been taken."

I tuned out the rest of the call. It was fucking hard enough hearing it aloud that Dusty had been taken. Someone had their hands on my woman, and they'd pay the price for it.

Looking at my hands, I wanted them wrapped around someone's neck for scaring Dusty.

No one had better harm her.

No one.

I'd fucking burn their place to the ground if they touched her—with them inside it. I needed to do something. The wait was killing me, tormenting me.

"Death."

"Don't call him. Just wait a little longer." He was like a fucking mind reader, but I didn't like his answer.

"If it was anyone else, I wouldn't, but I'm panicking here. This is Dusty."

"Country, it ain't worth owing that fucker anythin'. You know whatever he'll want will come at a bigger cost."

"Bigger cost than Dusty?" I roared.

Death stood from the couch. "You know I fuckin' didn't mean that. Say you get her back. That fucker will eventually want you to sell your own kidney or liver or fuckin' heart if he's in a bind with a client."

My jaw clenched as I stared him down. I knew he was right, but fuck, I'd be willing to try anything. If Blaze McCoy was a door I needed to open, I would. For Dusty, I'd do anything.

"All I'm askin' is for you to wait a little longer. Tech's our guy who can do anythin'. He'll get what we need."

"I will." Tech nodded from the computer as he glanced from one screen to another.

"Fuck. I know. Sorry." I scrubbed a hand over my face.

Death stepped up and slapped my arm. "I get it, Prez. I do."

Adrik and West appeared at the door. "You helped with West. I will help you and kill anyone who took your woman. I have men out looking."

"Thanks, Adrik." I nodded to West, who looked a little pale, but I knew he was a friend to Dusty.

"What about Henri? Would he know anything?" West asked.

Shit, I doubted it, but I'd try anything. Even listening to that guy.

"I'll check." I didn't have his number, but I presumed he would have taken Dusty's phone with him for safe keeping.

"Bonjour," he croaked through the phone. Since it was nearing two in the morning, it was no wonder he was asleep.

"Henri, Country, have you heard anythin' from Dusty?"

"Non, as you can see, I still have her phone. I was wondering who would call her phone at such a godawful hour. I thought it would have to be a creep... Not that I'm calling you a creep. Please don't kill me."

Sighing, I pinched the bridge of my nose. "I won't kill you, Henri, quit fuckin' sayin' that." Death and Tech snorted. "Listen, the cops might come see you tomorrow."

"Oh my God, you killed someone. I can't be an accomplice. I can't go to jail. I'm too good-looking... though, I could meet Mr. Right in there."

"Henri, shut the fuck up and listen. Do not speak until I say you can. Dusty's vet clinic got broken into. She got taken. We didn't get to her in time and had to ring the cops for the break-in, and they'll start looking into Dusty's disappearance." He whimpered into the phone. "We'll find her, Henri. We *will* fuckin' find her. I'll make sure of it. If the cops question you, act like you don't know anythin' happened to her. You and I didn't talk. Got it?"

"Oui. But who would take her?"

"Dead men, that's who."

"Can you... keep me posted? I have a friend that could help. I'll give him a call and—"

"I have somethin'," Tech announced, and my heart gave a nervous, excited, and scared stumble.

"Henri, I've got to go." I quickly hung up and went to stand behind Tech.

Tech pointed to the screen where two mug shots sat. "Dreads guy is named Jimmy Sarala. His friend with the skull tattoo is Brian Ivin. Both are in the Hotspot gang. Their boss goes by the name Yano."

"What do they deal in?" Death asked.

"Drugs mainly. Some trading when it suits them."

"Where are they?"

"Warehouse in the east. Head that way, and I'll get a direct location shortly."

"West, stay with computer guy," Adrik ordered.

"It's Tech," West supplied.

"Da, technology guy. I will go with Country."

"No—" West started but stopped when Tech shook his head. Tech knew it didn't matter what Adrik called him. He was there to help, and that was what counted.

"Adrik, do you have a weapon?"

"Da. Always."

"Death, grab the bag. We'll meet you at the car, and Tech, let the brothers know. We go in silent. Vehicles only."

"On it." Tech nodded.

It was time to get my woman back.

Dusty

THEY DRAGGED me kicking and screaming from the clinic, until I was hit over the head by something, and everything turned black.

When I woke next, I sucked in a breath, and my eyes fluttered open. Only to close again from the bright light and pounding headache. I tried to release the ache in my arms, but they wouldn't move from behind me. Panic pumped the blood through my veins faster, knowing I was restrained. Opening my eyes slightly, I glanced around. I was bound to a chair in the middle of a room. One that hadn't seen a cleaner in decades.

Like that matters right now, idiot.

Voices drifted through the closed door. "We hit the vet place like you said but ran into trouble, boss."

"What type of trouble?"

The handle jiggled. I quickly slumped, dropping my chin to my chest and closed my eyes. I only had one chance to regulate my breathing, but I wasn't sure I pulled it off since the noise of the door creaking opened shot fear into my system.

"Who the fuck is she?"

"She works at the clinic. Cleaner, I think. Was there when we broke in and… she was on the phone." The last part was said softly, like he didn't want to admit it.

I knew why when I heard a hard thump before something dropped to the floor.

"Who was she talking to? You'd better know, or I'll fucking kill you myself."

"We do," a new voice said. Brian. "He said his name was Country. President to the—"

"Diamond MC. You fucking fools," he bellowed, and

I couldn't hide the jolt to my body. "Ah, she seems to be awake." Footsteps approached before a hand snagged in my hair, and my head was pulled back roughly. My gaze landed on a Hispanic man dressed in jeans and shirt, with a jacket over the top. "Who are you to the Diamond MC?"

"N-No one."

My head shot sideways from the slap. "Don't lie to me, girl."

The side of my face burned as I slowly faced him. "They won't care I'm gone."

He read through the lie and slapped me again. "Try again." He shoved my head back and faced his men. "What did Country say? I need word for word."

Through my eye that wasn't swelling, I saw the men swallow thickly. It was the guy with dreads who supplied the answer. "He said that if we touched her, they'd hunt and kill us. Told us to leave her and take whatever we had, and he would have let the situation drop. But I knew it was a lie, boss. I knew he'd come, no matter, so I thought we could use her to keep them off our backs while we finish this heist."

Country. He would come and would bring the brothers with him to get me out. On that I didn't have a doubt. But would they find me in time before whatever the boss guy planned?

The boss laughed, shaking his head. "I don't ask for you to think. You should have left her where she was for them." He turned toward the door. "Now I'll have to figure something out for your fuckup. Expect to pay, boys." The door slammed after his exit, and I heard the lock slide into place.

Dreads ran for the door and tried the handle. "Fuck. Fuck." He spun back. "He locked us in."

Brian snorted. "No shit."

"He's going to kill us."

"Nah, he'll cut off some fingers to show his other employees not to screw up."

Dreads looked down at his hands. "Why the fuck aren't you fazed by this?"

Brian went to the wall and slid down to sit on the grubby floor. "It wasn't my idea to take her with us. I told you to leave her. I'll just tell the boss that."

"You'd throw me under the bus, just like that?"

"Yeah, Jimmy, I would. If it means I get to keep all my fingers and life, I'd do anything. You're new. You'll eventually learn to fight for yourself and only yourself in this world." Brian shifted his gaze to me. "You want to tell me who you are to the Diamond MC?"

Glaring, I shook my head. The movement made my face pinch in pain before the room spun. Whoever had hit me over the head had done a good job.

Brian huffed. "Didn't think you would." He glanced back to Jimmy, who was pacing. "Might do you good to get the answer from her to give to the boss. He might be more lenient."

Jimmy stopped, and so did my heart. He turned wide eyes from Brian to me and back again. "You think so?"

"Yep." Brian nodded, and I didn't like his sadistic smile at all.

With my feet untied, I kicked out at Jimmy as he approached. "No. Don't touch me. Don't listen to him. Please."

He grabbed my foot and flipped me back. I landed hard, and the old chair shattered under me. My hands stung while I tried to suck in a breath but gasped instead at the ceiling.

I couldn't get a breath. Tears stung my eyes as I tried. Hands grabbed my arm, and I was dragged away from the broken chair just as my lungs started working again, and I gasped for the air. It was then I heard laughter in the background. Brian.

Jimmy straddled my waist. Terror froze me for a moment until I started wiggling, kicking up, and kneeing his back.

"Stop," he snapped with a slap to my already aching face.

Stilling, I stared up at him.

I wanted to be home.

I wanted to be at the compound.

I wanted... Country.

Tears filled my eyes, and I bit on my trembling bottom lip, tasting blood.

Jimmy wrapped a hand around my neck. "Tell me who you are to them."

"A club girl," I whispered.

Brian laughed again. Jimmy looked over his shoulder. "What?" he snapped.

"A club girl? I doubt they'd care that much about pussy they could easily replace. There's something else."

"There's not. I promise I'm just a club girl."

Jimmy scowled down at me. "You're lying," he ground out before his hand tightened around my neck.

"No," I choked, wiggling, moving, trying to fight.

"Stop lying. Tell me now!"

"N-Not lying," I gasped.

"Jimmy," Brian called, and Jimmy's hand loosened enough for me to gasp in some breaths.

A weak whimper escaped me, filling me with shame. I wanted to be stronger. I'd thought I was. Apparently not, since all I wanted was to be saved and disappear from this painful nightmare. But I didn't get to close my eyes and wake up in my bed at the compound. I slipped further into a harsh reality with what Brian said next. "Fuck the answers out of her."

When Jimmy turned back and smiled, my stomach hollowed out. His hand left my neck to caress my cheek.

"You'd like that, wouldn't you? Probably used to being fucked into submission." He slipped down my body to sit on my thighs. His rough hands grabbed my breasts in a hard grip. "You going to talk when I give you my dick?"

"Yeah, I'm sure she will, Jimmy."

"Don't, please. Don't do this." A sob caught in my throat. Jimmy patted my cheek.

"You'll love it. I know you will, and then I can take information to the boss." He popped the button on my jeans. I rocked side to side to stop him, crying, begging. His hands ripped at my tee, exposing me. "Fuck, more than a handful. Come see, Brian."

I bucked and yelled until I felt a foot press down on my neck. Brian stared down at me, grinning. "Damn pretty titties. I might need a turn after you." He palmed his cock.

Bile rose, burning my throat. Tears glided down.

Jimmy's hand returned to my jeans and slid down the zipper. I couldn't move. I couldn't do anything.

No! I would do something, anything.

When Jimmy shifted up off me, I lifted my knee as hard as I could and caught him between his legs. He rolled to the side, groaned, and gripped his crotch.

"Fucking idiot." Brian laughed. His foot pressed harder down, cutting off my oxygen.

A door opened. "What the fuck is going on?"

The boss.

"Just trying to get answers for you, boss." Brian lifted his foot, and I wheezed with each panted breath. Jimmy groaned and sat up.

"Enough. We're getting rid of her. Get her out front now." He turned and left, leaving the door open.

Even with struggling for air, I rolled to my knees and tried for the door. Brian was there, though, gripping me under my arms and lifting me to my feet. He pressed himself into my back, grinding his hardness into my tied hands.

"Too bad, princess. We could have had so much fun." His hands slid around to grab my breast. "Get up, Jimmy." I heard shuffling before Brian dragged his nose up the side of my neck. "Yeah, heaps of fun. Maybe next time."

Another whimper left me, and I sagged back. His hands gentled, as if he thought I was giving in. I lifted my foot and stomped on his hard. He cursed, and I managed to pull from his grip to run for the door.

My hair was caught, and I was swung around to face Jimmy. I didn't see his fist coming before I was knocked out again.

CHAPTER TEN

Country

 e didn't fuck around when we pulled up to the warehouse. There were at least fifteen cars with brothers piled in them, and as soon as I climbed out, gun at the ready, the brothers followed. We walked right up to the front entrance. They'd know we were here. They'd know why. They'd better have answers.

I gave a chin lift to half of the brothers, and they scattered around the back. Adrik went with them. I didn't bother knocking. I tried the handle and flung the door wide since it was unlocked. Death gripped my shoulder when I went to walk in.

"Me first, Prez."

I ground my teeth together. Times like this, I hated

that the brothers thought my life was more important than theirs because I was president. "I got it, brother," I told him and stepped through before he could stop me.

A man stood in the middle of the warehouse with about twenty armed men at his back. I stopped just before him. "Yano, I take it?" He glanced from me to my brothers and down to the gun in my hand.

"Yes."

"You know why I'm here."

"I do. My men were mistaken when they took your club girl."

My brothers bristled in anger at the mention of Dusty being a club girl. She never really was, but now she was more, and she would always be.

"Where is she?"

"Not here."

My body locked, but I clipped, "What the fuck you mean?"

"Leave here and take the men responsible for taking her. I don't want a beef with you."

"What? No, boss," a man cried out, and I looked to the dead man with dreads. Beside him stood Brian. The other one I wanted a close word with.

"Where. Is. Dusty?" I bit out as my veins filled with fury. How could I be so close to having her back and now so far? This wasn't fair. It wasn't right. He'd pay for it as soon as I had answers.

Yano tensed. "She was taken by someone else."

"Someone stole from you?" I asked, knowing that wasn't it. The fucker was lying. Hiding something, and I'd make sure I knew what.

My phone started ringing. I held up a finger and then pulled my phone free. Dusty's number showed, so I knew it was Henri. He could wait. I pressed End Call and turned back to Yano to raise a brow.

Yano waved a hand around. "The semantics don't matter. I'm offering up the men who took her. Take them and we're even."

I forced a humorless laugh. "Yano. You don't know me or what we're capable of. For your sake. For your men's sake. Tell me who has Dusty."

"I don't know his name."

Lifting the gun, I tapped the end of the barrel against my temple. "I'm starting to get impatient, Yano, and that pisses me off." My phone rang again. Henri. I ended the call. He just had to fucking wait.

"I mean it, Country. I don't know his name."

"How did he take her?"

"Broke in while we were busy."

"Busy? With your hustle to hit multiple vet clinics in one night for the drugs?" Tech had found some information and rang me with it on the drive.

Yano's gaze narrowed. "How did you know?"

"Doesn't matter." My phone rang again, and I ground my teeth together. I handed it off to Death. "Deal with that." He took it and moved back behind our group.

"Country, I'm offering you the men in my gang who took the woman. That should please you. That should mean something. Hell, she's only a club girl. Would you want to go to war over some whore?"

Tension filled the room, mixing with the raging fury.

Torch shivered at my side and tapped the knives in each hand against his thighs. "Prez, let me, please. Let me have him for a minute. I'll get everythin' you need from him." His smile was a little manic, enough that it had Yano taking a step back.

Reaching out, I gripped the back of Torch's neck. "Soon, brother."

Torch started chuckling.

Turning my narrowed gaze back to Yano, I caught his nervous swallow. Death stepped up to my side. His hand rested on my shoulder, and I leaned into him. "Henri just gave us information you need to hear."

My heart skipped a beat at the tense tone Death used.

I held my hand out, and Death dropped the phone in it. "Torch, if any of them move, they're yours."

"You got it, Prez," he said gleefully.

Stepping back, I turned and moved behind the brothers. I lifted the phone. "What?"

"A friend of mine found out Dusty was taken by Yano, but he sold her to someone named Donald Spring."

Ice formed in my veins.

Donald Spring.

Fucking Duck. He'd been a member of the Diamond MC until we kicked him out for being a bigoted fuck when Wreck started dating Lucas. Obviously the beating he received wasn't enough of a lesson to mess with us.

"Christ."

"Death said you would recognize the name."

"I do."

"I'm having my friend find out an address. I'll call as soon as he has it."

"Give Tech a call. He's at the compound. He might have the information already. If not, he'll get onto it as well." A cry sounded behind me, but I knew my brothers would deal with it. Instead, I rattled off Tech's number to Henri.

"I'll call him now."

"Good, and Henri?"

"Oui?"

"Thanks for the help."

"I would do anything for Dusty."

"I know." I hung up and moved back through the brothers. Anger covered me like a heavy blanket as I stopped beside Death and Torch and eyed Yano.

He'd sold her.

What I needed to know now was what state she was in when he'd sold her. Why the fuck would Duck want her? Did he do it to get back at me? How would he know Dusty was important to the Diamond MC and not just a regular club girl?

"Tell me somethin', Yano."

"What?" His hand that held the gun twitched. Had he guessed I just found out he'd sold my woman?

Steadying my stance, I bellowed, "Why the fuck you sold my woman?"

People twitched, tensed, and some of his men backed up, looking over their shoulders for their friends. But they wouldn't come. There wouldn't be any type of backup because I knew my brothers were better. They would have restrained them easily in any way possible.

"Prez," Torch whined and shifted at my side.

I held my hand up. "Brothers," I yelled, and behind the men, my brothers appeared out of the shadows. The one who had most of the blood wasn't a brother but an honored member. Adrik gazed out as if bored.

Yano's men stilled.

At my nod, Torch's hand flicked, and Yano screamed as Torch's knives hit him. One in the chest, the other in his wrist, causing his gun to drop to the ground.

His men raised their weapons, but we were quicker. "Don't fuckin' move," I snarled. "Give us Yano and the two who took Dusty in the first place, and we'll leave. Someone else can take over the crew." At least then, whoever took over would know better than to mess with us.

Weapons were placed to the ground, and they held

their hands up. Torch clapped and laughed before he skipped over to Yano, who had fallen to his knees. Once there, he pulled the knives free and stabbed them in again. Yano screamed. He'd live long enough for us to have a word with him back at the compound.

"He would make a good Russian," Adrik commented.

Torch grinned up at him.

In the confusion, Brian thought he'd silently push back into the men. I lifted my gun, aimed, and shot him in the shin. He yelled, dropped to his ass, and gripped his wound.

"Do you agree with my terms?" I called.

When no one said anything, Torch rose, knives in hands, blood dripping off them, and snarled, "Answer him."

"We agree," someone said.

That was all I needed. I flicked a hand. "Load them up." I made my way back outside.

In the car with Death, Torch, and Adrik, I explained what we'd learned about Dusty.

"Dead Duck," Torch muttered, glaring out the window.

"Yeah, he'll be dead soon enough."

"Who is Duck?" Adrik asked.

"Former member. We kicked him out when he showed his bigoted side."

A rumble fell from Adrik. Out of all of us, he hated

bigots, even more so since his husband's parents had kidnapped their son and tortured him to "purge his sins." "I would like a word with him."

"You'll have it. As soon as Tech finds where he's situated."

My chest ached as pain spread through it. I thought I'd have my woman back safely, yet she was facing another cunt. I didn't know what Duck would do with her. Bile rose at the possibilities, but I had to push them back to stay strong. To stay hard.

"Your work in the warehouse," Adrik started, and I flicked a gaze back to see he was looking at Torch. He slowly glanced at Adrik. Torch didn't like a lot of people —not even all brothers—but those he did, he'd do anything for. "Where did you learn to throw like that?"

Torch studied Adrik. "Had to learn to incapacitate quickly." Torch didn't have parents. He had a grandfather who was a motherfucker and who Torch had killed at the age of fourteen by burning him alive. I'd found him on the street eight years later.

Adrik huffed. "I learned the same at a young age."

"Did you kill someone in your family too for being a fucking asshole?"

"Nyet. I killed others who would have harmed my family."

Torch grunted and went back to staring out the window. He'd be lost in the past for a while. It happened every time we had a situation where we had to kill. Torch lost himself to the bloodlust and became a different person than he usually was. His sentences were shorter and sharper because killing someone brought him so much glee—especially when he knew the man deserved it. In times like these, he became a killing machine, with one thing in his mind.

Death and I shared a glance. He would be thinking the same as me, that getting those two together wouldn't be a good thing.

Well, for everyone else.

Torch was loyal to me, and Adrik was with West. Thank fuck we had them on our side, because I wouldn't want to go up against them.

Shifting in my seat, I rested my head in a hand. Their conversation had helped push back some of the dread gripping my gut, but as soon as the silence hit, it reared its ugly head.

If Tech didn't have answers for me on Duck, I'd need a distraction and knew what the best one would be. As soon as we hit the compound and the brothers had those fuckers in the basement, I'd find out exactly what was done to Dusty and make them pay over and over.

Until they couldn't scream anymore.

DEATH, Adrik, and I hit Tech's room while Torch went to check on the prisoners. Before I could ask, Tech said, "Not yet, but soon."

As I deflated, West's gasp filled my ears, and he hurried over to Adrik, who cupped his husband's cheeks and brought his mouth up to his. "It is not my blood, moya lyubov'."

"Oh, okay."

Just like that, West accepted his answer without questions.

Dusty would have done the same. I knew it down to my bones. She'd be my other half like West was to Adrik. Like Courtney was to State.

I needed to get her back. To make her mine. But fuck, I was scared I'd never let her out of my sight again.

"I'm headin' to the basement." I fisted my hands at my sides, already wanting to harm the fuckers down there.

Tech grunted, not looking away from the computer. Adrik glanced up from West. "I will stay with West. You need me, call, but I feel the other one will do what I would." Meaning Torch.

"He will. Thanks for the assist, Adrik."

"The club helped with West." I understood what he meant; he'd have our backs because we'd had his. We were grateful for it and the help we could provide.

Out the door, I made my way down to the basement

with Death. When we hit the bottom, screams echoed down the hall.

"Bet it's Torch with his torch."

"Good."

We strode down the hall where State, Wreck, and Quake stood outside the room. They shifted, and I stepped through. The three men were bound and gagged to a chair each. Despite the gag, Yano's screams still rent the room as Torch aimed his blowtorch to the bottom of Yano's foot.

"Torch," I called.

He glanced over his shoulder before switching it off and straightening. "Just gettin' him warmed up for you."

"'Preciate it." I took a step closer and glared down at the pathetic piece of shit. "You wanna tell me why you sold Dusty?"

"Money."

Money. Always fucking money for greedy cunts.

"You could have called me. If you had and then thrown your guys under the bus with her waiting for me, I would have been lenient. Instead—" I leaned in and clipped loudly and slowly, "You. Picked. Not. To." He whimpered and started begging under his breath, blaming his men. Shaking my head, I stood tall and walked over to the wall. "Which is why I won't give a fuck when you die."

Turning, I swept an arm back and brought it forward

quickly. The axe embedded into Yano's neck, and we watched the life leave him as he choked on his own blood.

Torch laughed. "Guess the axe wasn't sharpened after we used it last."

The other two rocked, cried, and pleaded behind their gags. They would get it worse if they harmed Dusty in any way.

I nodded to Jimmy. Death moved over and pulled his gag free. "Please. Please don't kill me. I know we fucked up. We panicked. Please don't kill me."

"Then tell the prez what he wants to know, and things'll go easy," State said.

Jimmy nodded over and over. His alarmed gaze came to me. "What do you want to know?"

"Did you touch Dusty in any way?"

His face dropped all color.

My gut clenched as I ground my teeth together.

Torch moved in behind Jimmy and tugged his head back his hair. He tsked. "What did you do?"

A sob broke through. Snot and salvia rolled out as he cried and pleaded. Torch glanced at me, and I nodded. He lit his blowtorch and ran it over Jimmy's hair. Christ, it stank, but the screams were like a symphony to my ears.

"It was Brian's idea," he yelled.

Wreck threw a bucket of water over him.

Brian shook his head, eyes wide and full of terror.

Only I wasn't done with Jimmy. "What was?" I demanded harshly.

"T-To get answers out of her."

My gut twisted painfully.

"How?" Wreck bit out what I didn't want to, too scared at finding out what she'd been through. What she could still be going through.

Torch gripped his chin, leaned over him with the blowtorch heading for his eye. "Tell him."

"Beat her. We hit her and... a-and touched her tits."

Dropping my head back, I let out the rough, hard roar from deep within my chest.

When I straightened, heaving my breaths, Torch shut off his tool and stepped back. His smile was yet another crazed one.

"We make them suffer," I demanded of my brothers.

State stepped further into the room with Quake, and once he closed the door, the brothers were right there with me, making them pay in all the horrible ways we could think of.

We became what nightmares were made of.

Yet, even as they took their last breaths, I didn't feel it was enough.

A phone rang, and Death answered. "Yeah? Got it." He hung up. "We've got information on Duck."

I wiped the blood from my face with the back of my arm. "Let's go."

CHAPTER ELEVEN

Dusty

hen I woke again, my body protested, especially my head. I slowly blinked my one good eye open when I heard nothing and no one around me, only to close it again and whimper at the reminder of what those men did to me. Their hands I would never forget. Maybe it was wrong of me to pray that they'd get their just desserts, but I did anyway.

Reaching up, I gently ran my fingers over my swollen face and winced each time I touched a sensitive spot. There were many.

Opening my eye again, I blinked slowly as I looked at my hand and pulled the other one up to study them. They were unbound, but bruises and cuts covered them. A tingle of relief rolled through me at the thought of having them free. Sighing, I dropped them and squinted. I was in a different room from before. A bedroom. Perhaps it was a different place entirely. A single bed with ratty sheets and a bucket beside it filled the space. I didn't know how long I'd been unconscious, but when I glanced to the window, sunlight shone from between the gaps in the blinds. Groaning, I stood slowly from the floor. My back pinched and ached with every move.

They could have put me on the damn bed.

My head spun, and the room tilted. I gripped the end of the bed and waited for it to stop. My stomach churned at the thought of those men over me, and I gagged, but nothing came up.

A sob caught in my throat. I wanted to curl into a ball, but I couldn't. I had to do something instead of wallowing. I had to escape.

When my head settled enough, I took some unsteady steps toward the window. I looked down at my body. Seeing my tee split down the middle, I gagged again. My jeans were still undone as well. My throat closed as a stone of anguish filled it. With a cry, I gripped my tee and tried to pull it around to cover my chest, but my hands fumbled, and I kept losing the torn pieces. A tight-lipped wail escaped me, and I tugged the tee from my body, threw it to the ground, and glared at it.

Shaking my head, I sniffed and finished my slow walk to the window. I pulled the blind back, and the sunlight stabbed at my eye. I flinched away and took a step back. Raising my hand, I protected my eye from the light and glanced under the shade of my hand. A mewl fell from my lips when I saw the bars on the outside.

No. I wouldn't break down. I wouldn't give in.

Turning, I moved to the door, but of course it was locked. I pressed my ear against the solid wood, wincing when more pain sliced through my face. Still, I didn't move, needing to know if anyone was out there.

Nothing moved or shifted outside the room.

But then my heart gave a hard thump when I heard a door slam. Frantically glancing around the room, I searched for some type of weapon. A whimper escaped when I saw nothing. My throat thickened when foot-steps approached.

A key was inserted, and I quickly slid behind the door as it opened.

"Where…?" Someone stepped in, and even as my body and head protested, I jumped onto their back, wrapping my arms around their neck. The person dropped and rolled, digging fingernails into the skin on my arms and scratching down them.

Crying out, I loosened my grip and was shoved to the side.

For the first time, I took in the person and froze.

Only it wasn't for long, not when my anger boiled up and out.

"You fucking bitch!" I screamed and grabbed a

handful of Davina's hair to rip her head sideways before I planted my fist in her face. I didn't know how to fight, so I worked on instinct and prayed I didn't break anything on myself in the process.

She screamed and punched me in the stomach. I tugged her hair again, pushing her back to get my feet up, and kicked her in the side. She dropped, gasping in pain, and then quickly scooted on her ass away from me.

"What did you do?" I demanded.

A heavy set of footsteps raced down the hall, and a man stepped into the room, taking us both in. He moved to Davina and helped her up.

"You let her get the best of you?"

"Shut up, Duck."

Duck?

Why did that name sound familiar?

He wrapped a hand around Davina's neck and squeezed until her eyes widened and she gripped his wrist. He leaned in and snarled, "Watch what you say, whore."

He dropped his hand, and she panted. "This was m-my plan."

What was?

"So what? You came to me. I'm in charge." He turned to me, his gaze slowly running over my body. "You got a magic pussy to get Country tied in knots trying to find you?"

I didn't reply. Instead, I stood. "Where am I?" It was now obvious I wasn't with the men who'd taken me. It was almost laughable how grateful I was I wasn't around Jimmy and Brian again, because I could still feel Jimmy's hands on me. It didn't stop the tremor of unease raking over me, though. I didn't like the unknown. I didn't know what these two had in store.

If only I could remember where I'd heard the name Duck or know why Davina was here.

Duck's face soured as he seethed at me. "You ain't anythin' special. But at least you'll be a tool for some payback, bitch." He moved off to the door. "Don't worry where you are. You won't be alive long enough to care."

My throat closed off, and my body trembled at his words. I wrapped my arms around my waist and dropped to my knees, catching my sob. Still, a whimper escaped.

When Davina cackled, I looked at her through wet eyes as she sashayed up to Duck. "I knew I came to the right man."

Duck wrapped an arm around her to grab her ass. "I'm not stupid, bitch. You only came to me because word got out about you and no other club takes on dirty pussy." He shoved her out the door. "Go get the room set up and the camera."

Her smile was strained. Why was she here? What was the word that got out? Why was I even questioning anything when soon I wouldn't have anything to worry about?

Did I have enough in me to fight? And if I did, would I want to?

Was there a point?

I didn't know. Yet when I saw the door starting to close, I ignored the pain stabbing through my body and jumped up. I gripped the edge, pulled it back, and saw a startled Duck before I kicked him in the balls and punched Davina in the side of the face, and ran down the hall. I made it to the kitchen, which looked like something out of a horror movie, and glanced around for something, anything, to help, hearing the pounding footsteps of Duck.

My gaze locked on a frypan that still contained steaming oil. Just as Duck entered, I picked it up and turned, throwing the oil at him. He gripped his face and screamed. I held tightly to the pan and ran around him. I stumbled over the lifted dirty carpet in the living room and grabbed hold of the arm of the couch to stop from falling.

A pain-filled cry left me when my hair was snagged and ripped back, causing me to stumble. I yanked my hair free and spun to Davina.

"You're not leaving. Not after I got him to buy you."

Shock had me jerking backward. "Buy me?"

She laughed. "The crew you foolishly got taken by knew Country wanted you, so they quickly sold you on the dark web. If I hadn't been on there and saw the sale, then you wouldn't be here."

No, I'd be back in another nightmare of a place.

"Davina, I know you hate me, but why would you do this?" I swung an arm out and then pointed to the kitchen. "Why would he want to kill me? Why do you? I've never done anything to you."

Her face scrunched up in rage. I quickly held the pan in both hands like a tennis racket. She shook her head and crossed her arms over her chest. "You walked around the compound thinking your shit don't stink, looking down on all of us—"

"You're insane. I never thought that. I didn't care who slept with who."

"Yeah, right. If you had the chance to have Country on his back, you'd do him. He wasn't yours. He was mine. I wanted him as soon as I saw him. I wanted to be his old lady. I wanted to run the club beside him, but all he wanted was you."

"Bullshit." I backed up closer to the front door. Duck was still groaning in the kitchen, the sound of running water joining his pained moans. Knowing he could walk into the living room at any second for payback sent dread into my stomach. "He didn't and still doesn't want me." Keeping her distracted, I grabbed the door handle. "Are you blind? I had two nights over the span of years with that man. Are you seriously saying you read things wrong between Country and me, and now you want me dead?"

It was extreme, or she was unhinged. Both I expected. Turning the handle, I found it locked.

Fuck. What was I supposed to do now?

"I never read things wrong, Dusty. The girls talk, just not to you, and I know he hasn't slept with any of them since the last time you two were together."

Stilling, I swung my gaze from the front window to her. "What?" I breathed. "But you and he…."

"He never wanted me because I wasn't you."

My heart took off in its own dance.

Shaking my head, I snorted at myself. It didn't matter. It didn't change the fact these people wanted to see me dead.

"Davina, it doesn't explain why you want me dead because of Country not wanting to sleep with you."

"You stupid fucking cow. I want you dead because you've ruined *everything*. I hated you before, but now it's beyond that. Now they kicked me out, and no other club will take me on, all because of you. I *need* you to pay."

With death? I wanted to scream, but I didn't. Why was I even bothering talking to her? It wasn't like she'd listen to reason. She was crazy. Obsessed with Country.

Honestly, it was a waste of my time. I inched closer to the window. My plan to jump out the front window, hoping someone would hear or see and help, was going to hurt like a bitch, but it couldn't be worse than I'd already gone through.

Davina laughed. "What? No answer? You don't want to beg for forgiveness?"

"Forgiveness? It was you, Davina, who ruined your own life by the choices you've made. I'm just the easy target to blame." With that, I turned and went to jump—and Davina cried out as an arm wound around my waist, and I was flung backward to the floor. I screamed as more pain swept over me. I'd lost the pan. Opening my eyes, I went to search for it, but my gaze locked on Duck, standing over me panting. Half his face was red, swollen, and blistered.

He reached down, took hold of my hair, and dragged me toward the hall. Yelling and crying, I wrapped my hands around his wrist to try and pry it away, but I couldn't. Instead, I let go. The agony had me sucking in a breath as I tried to grab hold of the walls, the floors, anything to stop him.

Davina stood at the end of the hall with a smug smile on her lips.

A door opened. I grabbed the side as he went to drag me in. He kept tugging, and when I didn't let go, he kicked me in the side. My hands fumbled for the doorway, but it was too late. I lost purchase. Duck forced me into the room before he stepped out and closed it. When I heard the lock click into place, I curled into a ball and cried.

I'd failed.

I couldn't even save myself.

They were going to kill me.

But it couldn't be just because of Davina's infatuation with Country. Duck had to have a reason also. But what?

Did it matter?

I wouldn't get to see anyone again. I wouldn't laugh with Tech and Gun, tease Quake, dance with Courtney, drink with Eve, have coffee with Stracy, work with Henri….

Then there was Country. I would never have the chance to tell him I wanted him. To let him know my feelings were more than one night's worth.

I love him.

I couldn't deny it, and *if* I got out of this, I wouldn't anymore.

CHAPTER TWELVE

Country

*A*s I showered the blood from my body, I couldn't help but think about the first night Dusty and I were together. I'd spotted her from across the room where I'd been shooting the shit with brothers. She'd stood against the wall, but I didn't miss the way her gaze kept moving toward our group. I'd wanted to know who she was looking at and had wondered what she was doing at the club when Death caught my gaze and told me she was one of the new club girls. My cock had jerked behind my jeans.

I wanted her at first sight, which only intensified after talking with her. Only, after the fucking phenomenal sex we'd shared, I'd pushed her away. The moment we'd shared felt like she'd cracked my chest open and grabbed hold of my heart. The feeling had been too much, and I hadn't been ready to take those feelings on.

Now I wished I hadn't dicked around, thinking the club came first, as we'd been dealing with shit back then. I hadn't been ready to settle down either and was waiting for the other shoe to drop for her—when she'd see life outside of the club was what she'd needed. Only she'd stayed and became a rock for the brothers with everything she did around the place.

It wasn't until the second time together that I woke the fuck up and knew I had to improve my own life before I claimed her. But I let my own damn insecurities take hold, certain she wouldn't want to be with an old man like me. She deserved better. So I'd waited for her to make a move, for her to come to me. When she didn't, I'd allowed myself to think she didn't want more from me. It'd fucking hurt, which was why I'd let the women hang off me around her. I could never bring myself to fuck any of them, though. They weren't her. What I should have done was shove them aside and seek Dusty out to tell her she was all I wanted.

Regret boiled my blood every time I thought about how much time I'd wasted without her at my side.

Sighing, I scrubbed the last of the soap from my body, turned off the shower, and got out. I hoped by now Tech had found Duck. I needed to get my woman back. Needed to show her she was my everything and would always be until I took my last breath.

156 | LILA ROSE

After dressing, I made my way out into the common area. Brothers were scattered around the room on their phones, ringing people they thought would know where Duck was situated.

I moved through them all and headed toward Tech's room. In there I found Death, Adrik, Wreck, and State.

"Anythin'?" I asked.

"Give me five," Tech called.

"Prez." Saint stood in the doorway and thumbed behind him. "You'd better come out here." When he ducked back out and headed down the hallway, I followed, with Death, State, and Wreck at my back.

In the common room, the brothers stood around two forms. They shifted aside when I got there.

"I told you it wasn't a good idea to come here." Blaze fucking McCoy stood beside Henri, glaring at the people around him. Henri, meanwhile, shifted from one foot to another and glowered at Blaze.

"You'll do this, since you broke your blasted computer."

Blaze swung his dark gaze to Henri. "That wasn't my damn fault."

"Like I meant to trip on one of the million cords in your stuffy, tiny office and crash into your computer. Maybe if you cleaned up occasionally, it wouldn't have happened."

Blaze leaned into him. "I'm going to kill you."

Henri grinned at the devil. "No, you won't."

Blaze huffed, shaking his head. "Stupid fucking Frenchman."

I cleared my throat, and they both looked my way. Henri clapped. "Ah, good, it is Country. I have brought my source to help find Duck."

"Blaze McCoy is your source?" This wasn't fucking good.

"Maverick." Blaze smirked. "It's so not nice to see you."

"It's Country, Blaze. Fuckin' use it."

Henri glanced from us. "You two know each other?"

Death snorted. "Everyone knows Blaze and the illegal shit he deals in."

Grunting, I narrowed my gaze on Blaze. "We ain't havin' *him* on the case because we refuse to owe him any type of favor."

Blaze's smirk grew into a full-blown smile.

"He won't ask for a favor, since he owes me. Just let him in with Tech, and I'm sure they'll have Duck's location in seconds."

Blaze's smile dropped when Henri said Blaze owed him a favor. Made me really fucking curious why a man who dealt in deadly shit would owe a florist a favor.

"Blaze?" I had to get confirmation from his lips, else I'd kick him right out the front door.

He sighed and scrubbed a hand over his face. "Missing out on this fucking opportunity," he mumbled. With another sigh, he nodded, "Fine. I won't except anything in return for the help I'm about to give, from the Diamond MC or their families."

Thank fuck.

"Death, take him to Tech."

"This way." Death started back down the hall, and after Blaze shot Henri another glare, he followed.

Henri must have then realized he was alone in an MC compound surrounded by bikers. He kicked at the floor, gazed around everywhere, clasped his hands in front of him, then behind him. When he started whistling, I'd had enough.

"Henri, take a seat." I nodded to a table. "You want a drink?"

He glanced to the bar where one of the new prospects stood. "Does he come with the drink?" He winked, blanched, and his hands shot up in front of him, waving them. "I didn't mean—"

"Relax," Saint told him and led him over to the table.

"Oh, you were at the bar with your husband."

"That's right. What do you want to drink, Henri?"

The florist sat, shoulders sagging. "I could really go for a coffee."

I joined Henri at the table. "Make it two, prospect."

"You got it, Prez" was called back. State, Wreck, and Saint sat at the table with us, and all eyes were locked on Henri.

He fidgeted. "What?"

"How do you know Blaze McCoy?" State asked.

"Merde." His face heated like nothing I'd seen. Even his neck was red.

Saint chuckled. "Maybe we don't need to know."

Blaze was gay? But how did Blaze still owe Henri a favor? I didn't get it, and I wasn't sure I wanted to. I had other things to worry about. What I wanted more than anything was to know where Dusty was. To have her back. Fuck, even my skin itched in agitation because I was sitting on my damn ass doing nothing. Waiting felt like time passed slower.

Wreck shifted on his seat. "We do. For the club—"

"Wreck." Saint shook his head.

"We're not lettin' this go. How do you know Blaze, and why does he owe you a favor?"

"We fucked" was said from behind us. Blaze stood beside Tech. "What favors I owe are none of your goddamn business. Nothing will come back on the club. Here." He held out a piece of paper toward me.

Standing, I grabbed the paper, opened it, and read the address written on it. "Duck?"

Tech nodded. "I was close. Blaze helped me get it in seconds instead of minutes."

Relief had me gripping the back of the chair to stop from stumbling forward.

"Henri, stay here. Dusty might need you." When he nodded, I glanced at Blaze. "Stay or go, I don't care, but do not fuckin' touch anythin'. Prospects, keep an eye on him."

"He won't do anything," Henri said, but I still didn't trust Blaze.

The brothers stood around us after hearing what Tech said. They were waiting for the word. Waiting for me to command—that I was ready to get the fuck out of here and get my woman back.

"We ride," I yelled. The brothers shouted with me, and together we made our way outside. At my bike, I turned to the brothers. "We go in formation, with Gun in a car at the back. Park a block away and head in on foot. Silencers on. Death, State, Wreck, Saint, Gun, Tech, Quake"—who'd only arrived back shortly before— "with me. The rest go through the back. This is Duck. He'll plant a few tricks. Keep your eyes open, brothers, for trouble and the cops. If they're on our tail, we lose them."

My chest cracked as they shouted an affirmative.

"Let's get Dusty back," yelled Gun, and the brothers roared.

Soon, darlin'. Hang in there a little longer. We're comin'.

Dusty

Somehow, I fell asleep. When I woke, it was to the door being thrown open. The pain in my body screamed at me to stay still, but I had to push it back. I wasn't going to let him kill me without a fight.

I scooted back on my ass across the floor when Duck stepped in, his face still raw from the hot oil. Satisfaction rolled through me.

"Get the camera," he ordered.

I winced at his gruffness and reminded myself that Country and his men were looking for me. I just had to hold out for them to get there.

"It's right here." Davina shifted out from behind Duck.

"You know how to use it?"

She rolled her eyes. "It's not hard."

Duck's hand whipped out and backhanded her. She stumbled with a cry. "Don't fuckin' smart mouth me."

"S-Sorry, Duck."

Duck's gaze moved back to me. He took a step, and I used the wall at my back to help me get to my feet. My body shook, the panic forming like a dead weight in my stomach.

"Don't you see, Davina? He'll hurt you after this is done. He won't care about you. He—"

"Shut up," Duck yelled. His hand wrapped around my neck and tightened.

"D-Davina, please," I begged.

"Wait," Davina called, and my hope bloomed. "I haven't switched on the camera." The hope I had crashed to the floor.

I clawed at Duck's arm as he moved me in front of him by my neck. His other hand grabbed one of mine and pulled it down to my side.

"Keep fighting. Country will love to see the fire in you before I snuff your life out."

"W-Why?" I choked.

Duck laughed. "Because Country kicked me out of the club, and now he'll pay for disrespectin' me. Takin' those motherfuckers' side over mine."

As soon as he spoke, I remembered. Duck was the member who got removed because he'd started vocalizing his hate for gay people. Wreck had brought Lucas to the club that night. It'd happened the weekend after Country and I'd been together for the first time.

How psychotic and pathetic could this man be?

He angled down so we were nose-to-nose. "I thought Country was better. I was wrong. He'll see the mistake he made makin' me an enemy. I waited for the right moment. To take someone that'd hurt him over anythin', and that bitch tells me it's you."

"H-He is," I coughed out. His grip loosened a little, obviously wanting to hear my words, so of course I supplied them. "Country is better. He got rid of *you*."

Duck screamed in my face before he flung me to the side. I hit a wall and slid down. He grabbed my foot and dragged me out of the room, back into the living room, where a plastic sheet was laid on the floor. Panic and fear shot through me, stilled me for a beat before I doubled my efforts to stop him. My nails broke as I tried to dig them into the hardwood floor to stop him. Only it didn't work.

A scream built, and I let it out as I kicked at him with my other foot. He dodged and punched it away with a laugh. My gaze caught on Davina, who stood with a small smile on her lips as she lifted the camera higher.

The red light blinked at me.

This was it.

This was how I was going to die.

Duck held me down as he straddled my waist and pressed a knife to my throat. He looked up at the camera. "Country, bet you didn't know what fear was until I bought her." He removed the knife as he bent and went to lick me. Before his tongue made contact, I jerked my head up as fast as I could, hoping I hit the mark and did some damage. Pain lanced through my head, but through my uninjured eye, I peered up at him, gasping in satisfaction. I'd hit his nose. He dropped the knife and cupped his face as blood poured.

Never had I moved so fast, shoving him aside and moving out from under him.

With adrenaline pumping through my veins, I picked up the knife and saw the whites of Duck's eyes as he realized his mistake. My arm moved instinctively, shoving the blade into his stomach. Wide-eyed, I froze, looking on in terror as he groaned, dropped to his side, and glanced down at the embedded knife.

"No, no, no. This is not how it goes," Davina yelled, cutting through my frozen limbs. But I couldn't look away from the blade.

I went to speak, not quite sure what I planned to say, but jerked when Duck reached for me. I scooted back, panicking when he got a hold of my ankle. I kicked at him with my other one until he half rolled on it. Behind me, I scrambled for purchase on something solid. I grabbed the leg of the couch and pulled, my body screaming at me to stop.

I couldn't.

I wouldn't.

Not if it meant more time for me. I was not prepared to die like this.

Glass shattered, wood splintered, and Davina wailed, dropping to the floor as I covered my head and curled into myself on my side.

Shouts, footsteps, and noise filled my ears, but I didn't dare look out. I didn't know what else was coming.

A roar filled the room. My body shook harder from it. The pressure on my legs lifted, a moan echoed, but still, I didn't move, didn't look. I heard Davina crying, sobbing, saying something I couldn't work out.

Beside me there was a rough voice that snarled, "Fuck me, fucking hell."

My whimper escaped when something thumped onto the ground next to me.

A hand touched my shoulder, and I curled deeper into myself, a terrified mewl slipping through my thinned, sore lips.

"Darlin'."

Stilling, I listened to see if I'd imagined it or not.

"Dusty, baby." A featherlight touch appeared on my back.

Uncurling, I removed my arms from around my head and looked up at the most beautiful sight. I didn't care that Country's expression was dark with a firm frown and hard eyes. He was here.

Country was here.

He sucked in a sharp breath, and I heard cursing around me as he took in my face. I ignored it all and slowly reached out to him.

Country quickly slipped his palm in my grip.

Licking my dry lips, I murmured, "You're here."

A noise rumbled out of him, the sound making my heart speed up. He dipped to kiss the back of my hand. "I'm here, darlin'." His eyes looked a little glassy, and I wondered why. He was tough. He was Country. He didn't have a reason to cry.

His forehead touched the back of my hand as a blanket was placed next to me. "Baby," he uttered to me before he snapped his head up and ordered, "Take them both in. Wreck, get Lucas to meet us at the compound." He grabbed the blanket and placed it over me.

"Country, please, I didn't do anything. Duck had me captive," Davina cried.

Country's gaze dropped to me.

With a raspy voice, I said, "She got Duck to buy me."

"You fuckin' cunt," Gun yelled. Saint held him back as State tied her arms behind her and led her out of the house.

"Hey, vroom, vroom." I glanced to my side to see Quake and Tech kneeling. "We're gettin' you home. Death's gettin' the car."

They all looked so sad.

"I-I'm sorry."

"What for, baby?" Country asked.

Suddenly tired, I looked back at him and blinked. "Sorry for this mess. For upsetting you all."

"Fuck, darlin', don't apologize." He brushed my hair back, and my eye closed at the gentle touch. "Tech, Quake, get your rides. Torch, organize the brothers to do a clean."

Torch's head tipped to the side, his dark and haunted gaze on me. As he tapped the knives in each hand against his thighs, he winked. "Good to have you back."

I tried for a smile, but it pinched too much. "Thanks."

"Torch," Country called. "I'm gonna be busy at the compound. You're with State and Death for questioning. I'm finishin' it, though."

Torch straightened with a bright smile. "Yes, Prez."

"We're goin' in also," Tech said, thumbing to him and Quake.

Most of what they said went over my fogged and exhausted brain, but I got the sense they were talking about who would be in the room with Duck and Davina. I waited for the panic, the disgust, but I couldn't find it in me to care what happened to them, not after everything I'd been through.

With a nod, Country grunted, and Quake leaned in, saying, "See you soon, sister." My heart clenched. He'd stood and moved to the door. Tech followed after giving me a small smile. Then I heard, "Gun's here with the car."

Country looked down at me. "I'm gonna pick you up, darlin', and it's gonna hurt."

"I know," I uttered. But this pain meant I was safe. It meant I was going home. So I'd take it all. Country gently slid his hand under my shoulder and had me sit up enough to wrap the blanket more around me. His other hand went under my knees, and when he lifted, I bit down on my bottom lip and closed my eye to try and block Country from seeing the agony in them. He held me against his chest and kissed my forehead as he left the house. Men surrounded us, blocking us from any neighbors, all the way to the car where Country slipped into the back with me still in his arms.

"I've got you, darlin'," he said softly, gazing down at me.

My breath hitched, my bottom lip trembled, and I gripped the neck of his tee, curling into him more as the tears fell.

His lips pressed against my temple. "I've always got you, Dusty. From now on."

I didn't know what he meant, but all I cared about was that he was here. I was in his arms and out of the nightmare.

Country held me all the way home as I cried into his chest.

I knew he'd come. I just knew.

CHAPTER THIRTEEN

Dusty

ountry carried me from the car and into the compound, with Saint running to open the door. I blinked up at the night sky as a cool breeze touched my feet. I hadn't even realized I'd lost my shoes at some point or when they'd been taken from me, but it was nice to feel the air against me. My eye closed again. I was drained from being unable to stop crying in the car. It was the solace of knowing I was safe and protected that had me finally steeling my emotions just before we pulled into the parking lot at the compound.

A gasp sounded. "Dusty, mon amour."

Opening my eye, I saw Henri hovering close as Country kept walking. Where to, I wasn't sure.

"Henri? W-What are you doing here?"

His hand covered his mouth when he got a good look at my face. I knew I must have resembled some type of monster. Tears welled in his eyes. "I came to help."

"Henri," I whispered, my heart once again clenching.

"You can talk to her soon. Lucas," Country bellowed.

Footsteps pattered the ground. "I'm here."

Country grunted as he took me to the hallway that led to the brothers' bedrooms. I winced when I tried to scrunch my face as confusion swept in. He didn't stop until he had me in his room, on *his* bed.

When he stepped back, Lucas moved in. I expected Country to leave. Instead, he moved around the mattress to sit on my other side.

Lucas's lips thinned as he looked to Country. "It might be best if you left for now."

"No."

"Country," I started, holding my hand out to him. He took it, kissing the back. "Why don't you go see how things are going?"

His jaw clenched. "If you want me to go, I'll do it, but I'm stayin' if you're all right with it."

If he wanted to stay, how could I say no?

"Okay." I tried for a smile, but it hurt. Honestly, since the adrenaline left my body, I ached all over and wanted to cry again.

Lucas sighed. "Dusty, there's questions I'm going to ask that Country may not like."

Knowing what they were, I nodded. Licking my dry lips, I looked to the wall. "It's fine. They, um, they didn't rape me." I couldn't look at Country, not when his hand gripped mine tighter. "T-They touched me, beat me... the first people, but didn't do *that*. Duck just... he, ah, hit me and dragged me around."

"All right. I'm going to hook you up to fluids as you're dehydrated, but do you want a shower first?"

A shower sounded like heaven.

"Yes, please. I-I can go to my room and—"

Country's hand squeezed mine. "You'll stay here."

"But—"

"Here."

Blowing out a breath, I relaxed into the bed more. I didn't want to argue with him. I was tired, dirty, and sore. "All right." I glanced back to Lucas and blushed. "Would, ah, just in case, would you be able to help me? Or I could ask Henri."

"I will," Country stated.

"Country—"

"Not anythin' I ain't seen before, darlin'." He grinned, only it quickly faded when I caught his gaze running over my injuries.

Lucas cleared his throat. "Let me just check for a concussion before I give you any type of pain meds."

"I did sleep at that house," I told him.

"That's good, but humor me and let me do my job, yeah?" His smile was gentle.

"Okay."

Country watched as Lucas got to work, asking me questions and checking me over. He didn't stop at testing for a concussion. He ran his hands over me, pressing, feeling. Each touch Country huffed at with a glare.

Lucas hummed under his breath, pulled back, and looked up to Country. "Bruised ribs, cuts, scrapes, bruises in other places." He glanced back down at me, and I wondered if he could no longer handle looking at Country. If that was the case, I understood completely. With each injury Lucas listed, Country looked scarier and scarier. "What I'm more concerned about is your fractured cheekbone. I'll look into it more after your shower, but you might need surgery."

The fracture explained the swelling and pain in the right side of my face and my inability to open my eye.

He reached into his bag and brought out some pills. Country gently placed my hand on the bed, stood, and went to the small fridge to grab a bottle of water. After I took a couple of pills, wincing the whole time, Lucas stood. "I'll do some research. We might need an X-ray to determine which way is best." He faced Country. "I can sneak her into the doctor's office I'm currently doing my residency in."

"We'll do it after she's rested."

Lucas frowned. "The sooner, the better."

"At least let her shower and the pain meds kick in."

"Of course." He glanced from Country to me and back again. "Just don't eat anything as yet. I know you must be hungry, but if we can get in tonight, it'll be better doing the surgery on an empty stomach."

"She hasn't eaten in—"

"It's fine, Lucas." I blinked up at Country. "I'm fine."

His jaw clenched again. "Thanks, Lucas. Can you find her a change of clothes? Try Eve."

Lucas nodded. "Just take it slow in the bathroom."

"I will," I promised before he walked from the room. His leaving reminded me who was going to be helping me in the shower. My face heated and my belly tingled. Surprise coursed through me at my reaction. I grabbed the sheets, considering my body's reaction to the thought of Country naked and helping me.

If I was a man, I would be sporting a semihard cock.

How ridiculous was that? After everything I'd been through. After how much pain I was still in, I was reacting to the idea of a naked Country.

Country removing his cut had me clenching the bedsheets harder. Wide-eyed, I watched as he hung it over the back of a chair and then pulled his tee from his body. I swallowed thickly. He undid and pushed his jeans down after kicking off his shoes and removing his socks. It left him in his black form-fitting cotton boxers.

He moved over to his bed and helped me stand. A whimper escaped me.

"Sorry, darlin'."

"Not your fault."

His jaw clenched. "If we had—"

"Don't, please."

"All right, sugar." He made sure I was steady enough on my feet to help remove my jeans and underwear. I expected to be more aroused or embarrassed, but the meds hadn't kicked in yet, and the pain was taking away any other feeling.

He straightened and reached around me to unhook my bra. A tick started in Country's temple when he eyed my other bruises and cuts. He lifted a wrist and kissed the inside before helping me into the bathroom that was joined onto his room. He flicked on the switch and had me rest against the sink while he started the water.

I couldn't stop watching him. Every move reminded me I was home. I was back at the compound where I was meant to be. I knew this like I knew tomorrow would come. This was my home. These were my people, my family.

Anything else I would think of later. Especially why it was Country taking care of me and not someone else. Maybe it was the guilt of someone in his club being treated badly, or was it something more?

No. Think about it later.

He turned and rested his arm around my waist, walking me into the shower. The steam billowed out.

"Try the temp, darlin'."

Reaching out, I flicked my fingers through the water.

"It's perfect."

Country grunted. He shifted so the full spray of the water beat down on me. Closing my eyes, I let out a long sigh. It felt wonderful. So good, in fact, tears slipped out and a sob caught in my throat where I made a godawful sound. In the next second, I was in Country's arms.

"Baby, you're safe. You're home."

"Country" was all I could manage on a broken sob.

"I got you. I got you, darlin'." His lips pressed against my wet hair.

I pressed my uninjured cheek onto his chest and sucked in a shaky breath. My body trembled as the thoughts of what happened, what I'd been through, ran through my mind.

"I got you," he said again softly, running his hands up and down my back.

He did.

He had me, now as well as before.

Country meant so much to me, but no way could I tell him. Not yet anyway.

Sucking in a shuddering breath, I gripped his waist and just let myself feel him against me. It was a comfort I desperately needed. Having him close reminded me of Davina's words—that he hadn't been with anyone since the last time we'd been together, which was over six months ago.

Why had he stopped sleeping with the other

women?

Though, the knowledge was a cool balm to my heart.

"I'm here, darlin'. Always will be."

God, he was warming me on the inside, like the water was on the outside. He didn't know it yet, but he was mine. Once I knew I'd be okay from everything that had been thrown my way, I would make him understand we would be perfect together.

"Gonna wash your hair, baby."

My breath hitched, and my body shivered when he ran his hands over my hair, massaging shampoo into it. How he took care of me had me falling in love with him even more.

Please let me get through this.

Please let me have him.

Please.

Having made it out of my nightmare, I wanted to dream of a life with Country. Not only did I want to dream it, but I wanted to make it a reality.

I was home.

I was meant to be here.

With him and this family.

The thought of it being taken from me almost took my legs out from under me. Country wrapped his arm around my waist.

"You're good, baby. It's gonna be all right."

I believed him, and every word, every gesture he offered made me feel safe.

Country rinsed out the shampoo and applied the conditioner. After he was done, I leaned against the wall while he softly washed my body. Seeing him on his knees taking care of me brought another sob forward.

Silently he stood, wrapping me into him once again. If he wasn't careful, I wouldn't allow him to let go, wanting to be in his arms always.

He eased me out of the shower and dried me off, even my hair, before wrapping a towel around me and taking me back into his room.

Courtney straightened from the bed, and I noticed she'd changed the sheets. When her eyes landed on me, her mouth dropped open, and a mournful sound escaped as tears filled her eyes. Eve walked into the room at that moment and stilled.

"Those motherfucking dickheads of a whore," she yelled before dropping the clothes she held to the bed to grip each side of her neck. "I'm gonna bring them back from the dead and kill them again and again and again." If she could, I believed she would.

"I'm okay," I whispered.

Country kissed my temple. "You will be, darlin'."

"Court," Eve snapped. "Go and hug her. I'm gonna go find something to stab." She took the few steps to me and took my hand, giving it a squeeze. "You're home."

"I am."

"You'll stay *home*."

"I, ah—"

"She will," Country stated gruffly.

Eve looked up at him, studied him, and nodded. When she left the room, Courtney took her place and gently leaned in to kiss the good side of my face. Her hands on my shoulders applied pressure.

"I'm so sorry this happened. You're safe now."

Tears built as I nodded. "I know."

"If you need anything, I'm here."

I sniffed. "Thank you."

Courtney looked up at the man beside me and nodded once before she left, closing the door behind her.

"Come on, baby, let's get you into somethin' comfortable so you can rest." He led me over to the end of the bed and moved a tee and jeans to the side. There was a nightgown underneath the small pile. Noticing it was a little see-through, I held my breath at the same time Country grumbled something. "Sit down, darlin'. I'll grab somethin'." He helped me to sit and went into the walk-in closet. It was then I realized I ached a little less. When he returned, he wore a new pair of boxer briefs and held one of his tees. "This'll be big and long enough." He placed it on the bed and picked up the panties I hadn't noticed. He knelt on the floor, and my face warmed when I placed each foot in the holes. I stood, and he slipped them up my legs and under the towel as he straightened.

"Thank you," I uttered.

He shook his head. "Don't thank me, Dusty. It's nothin'."

"It is. Your help means a lot." *You mean a lot.*

He dipped in and pressed his lips to my forehead but said nothing. Instead, he picked up his tee and slid it over my head, keeping it away from my face. I pushed my arms through the holes. Country had been right; the tee was baggy and long, landing midthigh. It was perfect, mostly because it was his.

He didn't know yet, but he wasn't ever getting this back.

Country made a noise in the back of his throat, and before I could look up from his tee, he had his arms wrapped around my shoulders. He kissed my temple and ran a hand up and down my back. "Let's get you into bed for some rest before Lucas comes back."

"I could go to my—"

"No."

"But—"

"No. Rest in here, darlin'. You ain't got anythin' in that room since you took it all, but we'll talk about that another day."

"Okay," I whispered.

He gently turned me and, with a hand on my lower back, he made sure I was steady to walk to the left side of the bed. I noted it was the furthest away from the door. He pulled back the blanket and helped me slide in with a hand to my upper arm.

The drugs, along with exhaustion, were kicking my butt. I lay back and blinked tiredly up at him. He covered me in the blanket and started to move away from the bed.

"Country," I called. When he faced me, my cheeks heated. "Can… will you, um, stay?"

His gaze softened. "Darlin', I was already gonna stay. Just putting your towel in the bathroom, and I'll be back." He winked and carried on after turning out the light and leaving the bathroom one on.

It felt like a long time since my heart hammered in my chest that didn't have anything to do with fear. Country climbed into bed and scooted close. He rested a hand on my belly while gently placing his forehead against the side of my head.

It was silent for a while, both of us breathing softly. But then his voice rumbled into my ear. "Darlin', need you to call me Maverick from now on."

My good eye sprang wide. "Why?"

"Will you just do it—for me?"

"Yes," I said instantly. I would do anything for him. Having permission to use his Christian name meant so much to me, making me think that I wasn't alone in wanting more between us.

And with that peaceful thought, I drifted off to sleep with a smile on my face as Maverick glided his fingers up over me.

CHAPTER FOURTEEN

Country

a soft knock sounded on the door. I slowly tore my gaze away from Dusty and lifted my head to order quietly, "In."

Wreck stepped inside with Lucas, who shuffled on his feet. "Tech's bringing in an X-ray machine. I don't know where he got it from, and I doubt I want to. But where should we set it up?"

"Dusty's old room. Take the bed out to fit it if needed."

Lucas nodded and glanced up at his husband before giving him a quick kiss and leaving. Wreck stayed. "Want to talk in here or out there?"

"Meet you out there." I didn't want Dusty to wake and hear anything she didn't need to. Though, I was reluctant to leave her because, fuck, she'd been through hell. It crippled me to know and see the damage it caused my sweet, caring, and humble woman.

Sighing, I withdrew my arm from over her, and she let out a little sound in her sleep as if she missed my touch. Sometimes I really did fucking hate being president. But if this was about those cunts in the basement, I wanted to know.

I didn't bother dressing as I headed to the door. Wreck shifted back so I could partially close the door, leaving it open enough to hear anything.

"They talk?"

Wreck grunted. "Davina's involved in the black market. Sick shit, like she'd act gettin' snuffed on film, but then her body is replaced by an already dead one at the end."

With my face screwed up in disgust, I snarled, "How the fuck did we not know this?"

"It was before she even started here, and it wasn't traceable to her real life. It was how she saw Dusty up for sale on the dark web. She remembered conversations about Duck gettin' booted and went to him. Knew he'd want payback, and he'd been biding his time to make you suffer. Prez, shit, he was gonna kill Dusty and send you the video of it."

My blood boiled. I wanted to march down into the basement and slice his fucking throat open, but that'd be too easy for him. He deserved to suffer.

"Wreck, I'm gonna ask you somethin', and I want you to be totally honest with me. I'm gonna make Duck pay, but I don't want him dead. I want him in pain over and over again. If I go too far, will you allow Lucas to heal him so I can do it again?"

Wreck's jaw clenched. "I don't want that for Lucas."

"Understood."

Lucas was a soft soul, and really, I shouldn't have asked, but my desire for revenge was strong. It sucked I'd already killed the others who'd harmed Dusty. Wished I could bring them back to do it over again.

"Keep him alive for me then. I'll come down when I can."

"What about Davina?"

That was another problem. Our club wasn't one that hurt women. We'd blacklist them and send it to other clubs to warn them about the bitches we got rid of and why. But to harm one was on another level.

Except Davina deserved to hurt.

Lifting my gaze, I ordered, "Ring Eve and Tech. Get them up here." Wreck pulled his phone free. This was only one option that formed. If they weren't in it, I'd speak to Blaze to see if anyone was interested in some body parts, but they'd have to get them themselves. Hell, I could even offer up Duck. Request Duck was alive while his organs were being removed.

Shit, that'd be the better move. Keep our hands clean. Well, they were already dirty, but this was what they got for fucking with the wrong woman. *My woman.*

Reaching out, I grabbed Wreck's shoulder. "Cancel that thought. Want a meeting with the brothers as Lucas checks over Dusty's cheekbone. Get Tech to send out a call for the brothers to hang about until that happens."

"On it." He nodded. "Tech, hey—"

"Country!" was shouted from my room, freezing my blood.

I bolted inside and moved over to the bed, where Dusty ran her hand on the empty side. "I'm here, darlin'." I slid under the blanket and took her hand, pressing it against my chest.

"I-I'm sorry."

"Don't apologize, baby. You need me; I'm there. Did you have a bad dream?"

"Yeah," she breathed, scooting closer to rest herself beside me. My gut twisted, I fucking hated this shit playing on her mind in her sleep. I glanced over when I heard movement near the door and caught Wreck quietly closing it. They'd come get us when the X-ray machine was set up. I'd have to thank Tech a damn million times over for getting one. Saved us breaking into the medical clinic, but mostly, it meant Dusty didn't have to travel. It wasn't like it'd go unused. The brothers sometimes got injured when we were in a situation.

"I'm here, sugar. Right here." I kissed her forehead,

and she let out a shuddering breath. "You need more pills?"

"Not yet."

"All right. You need anythin', you let me know."

"Just your warmth. I feel cold all over."

I shifted closer, hooking a leg over hers and wrapping my arm around her. "I've got you, Dusty." She hummed under her breath, relaxing more into me. "Noticed you didn't call me Maverick, baby."

"Huh? Oh, um, yeah, it might take some time to get used to."

"Got all the time in the world, darlin'." For her, I had every second of every damn day. She didn't know it yet, but things had definitely changed between us. As soon as I knew she'd cope with the knowledge, I'd let her know. I could be patient.

I thought she'd drifted back to sleep until she whispered, "Maverick."

It was the wrong time for my dick to throb at hearing my name come from her mouth. "Yeah, Dusty?"

"I just wanted you to know I appreciate you being here."

"There's no place I'd rather be. I fuckin' *hate* what you got put through." *And I'll be at your side for the rest of our lives to make sure nothing like that happens again.*

She patted my chest. "I know you do. I know how the brothers get angry if something unjust happens to someone in the club."

It wasn't just that. "Darlin'" was all I could manage to say. If I said more, I'd end up telling her how important she was to the club. To me. Not only did the brothers see her as a sister now, but she was going to be my old lady. The president's woman. She was more important than my own life. The brothers knew that if anything more happened to her, I'd lose my shit like an atom bomb going off, and no one would want to go against my wrath.

"Do I need to get ready to go to the clinic?"

"No, baby. Tech got us an X-ray machine. We'll do it here as soon as it's set up."

"Tech got an X-ray machine?"

"Yeah."

"How did he get an X-ray machine?"

"Fuck knows, but it'll come in handy."

A small laugh fell from her lips, and Christ, it was good to hear.

"It'll come in handy in the future," I added, not wanting her to think she was the cause of getting one.

"I'm sure it will." I could hear the smile in her voice. "It's lucky you have Lucas as well."

"Yeah, it is. Even if Wreck didn't switch for him, we'd at least have him through Saint being his brother." She hummed under her breath. "You in pain, darlin'?" Talking probably didn't help either. Fuck, I should have considered that already.

"A little."

"No talkin', baby. It won't help the pain." Kissing her temple, I started to shift back. "I'm gonna get Lucas here to give you more pain meds."

"Wait. Don't go yet. Please."

I didn't like she was in pain, but how was I supposed to say no to her when she wanted me close? I moved back into her on my side and blindly reached back for my phone.

Me: **Wreck, get your man here. My woman needs more meds.**

Wreck: **He's nearly done here. Wants to scan her ASAP. He'll probs operate after if needed. Give her something stronger.**

Sighing, I dropped the phone to the bed. "Lucas'll be here soon. Just rest, baby. No talkin' for me." I felt her small nod. "Good. Now I've got you quiet, I'm gonna let you know somethin'." Her hands gripped mine between us. "Never been scared like I was when I *heard* them take you." She stilled, lifting her gaze through one eye to mine. "When I was young, I used to live out in the country, and one night I decided to take a walk through the woods that surrounded our house. I was about five and thought it'd be cool to see some fireflies, like the ones I'd seen on the television that day, only I didn't know there wouldn't be any in our area.

"It was too late to realize they wouldn't light up the woods for me because I was already lost. I hadn't even told my parents where I was going, just slipped out of the house as I knew they'd try and stop me. I've never cried as much as I did that night. Every noise shot fear into me. But thinkin' back on that night, the fear was nothin' compared to what I felt when they took you."

Fuck, had I said too much? Her soft, emotion-filled "Maverick" gripped at my chest. But when she touched her fingers to my bottom lip and chin, I got the strangest sense that she liked what I'd said. Still, just in case I'd messed up, I shifted the subject, but wanted her to know more about me, knowing it was what two people who were into each other did.

"Anyway, when I started with the Diamond MC, they picked the name Country because it was where I was from. It's not as cool as some of the brothers', but it meant somethin' to me. It's where my life started and where I buried my parents after they passed." I'd always liked the name. "You're probably wonderin' how I got into the club in the first place? I'll tell you." Absently, I ran my hand up and down her back. It reminded me of the sight of her in my tee, and fuck, that was a damn good picture. "I'd moved this way around seventeen, after losing my parents, and had to live with my pa. At first I was a little shit, had many issues, and didn't even want to finish my last year of high school.

"Pa wasn't havin' it." I chuckled at the thought. "He marched me into school that first day and said if I didn't stick it out, I'd lose my chance at havin' my own ride. He'd known I'd been eyeing off his since I got there, and

I wasn't gonna lose my chance of him helpin' me get one. Luckily I stuck with school, because that's where I met Death and State. State's a few years younger than us and was always followin' Death and me around like a lost little puppy. Fuck, don't tell him I said that. He'll kill me."

Her small smirk was everything.

"Yet, we bonded like brothers, and as we grew older, we began to plan where we wanted our futures to go. We knew college wasn't for us. It wasn't until Pa told us he was a member of a biker club called the Diamond MC that we all had a direction. He hadn't mentioned it or taken me to the clubhouse before, telling me I hadn't been ready. He was right. But after he'd said it, it was like a lightbulb goin' off in our heads. We knew we wanted to be a part of that club. I'd never wish a different life for me. What we've grown together is a big fuckin' family of love, trust, and respect. But like all families, we have our ups and downs. We get mixed signals and fuck up. It's how it turns out in the end that matters." Kissing her hair, I rested my hand at the back of her neck. "Sorry, darlin', I'm just dribblin' on, and you probably want to sleep."

"I like it," she whispered between us.

My chest puffed up as a damn giddy feeling slid in. My woman liked knowing things about me. Liked wanting to get to know me. Yeah, we definitely had a future together.

"Good," I grunted. "But no more talkin'."

She huffed out a laugh.

"Or that," I warned with a light tone. I stilled when she brought my hand she'd been gripping up to kiss my fingers.

My heart was hers.

She controlled it and how it beat harder in my chest.

It was hers completely.

Always.

Clearing my throat since it thickened with those damn giddy emotions, I used my other hand to slide down her back. Stopped just before I reached her ass.

"I'm gonna tell you a few things you might not know about me." She hummed and pulled my hand closer to her. "I was eighteen when I lost my virginity." Her head angled back to show me her good eye wide. "Yep. I'd been homeschooled with my parents, so when I got to Pa's, everything changed. I walked around with a constant boner for a few good weeks, since there were so many pretty girls at school." I grinned at her laugh until I caught her wince, which she tried to hide by dropping her head back down. "Shit, I'll try to not make you laugh. Sorry, darlin'."

"I like it,' she said again, just as softly.

"All good, baby. I'll think to talk on other things. Don't want you in more pain than you already are." I traced my fingers back up and over her shoulder, gliding fingers up and down her arm as I thought of things.

"You could say I went a little wild when I moved in with Pa, another reason he didn't mention the club. For a few years, he didn't know what to do with me, but no matter what, he always had my back. He never liked how remote my parents lived, so I guess in a way, he let me have my fun until he reined me in when I hit twenty-two. It was around that age when Death, State, and I joined his club and learned Pa was the president. He'd told us one night that it was he who'd come up with the name Diamond MC. He picked it because diamonds could cut down anything, and he wanted his club to be that strong." A pang hit my chest when I thought about Pa.

"Lost my parents to a landslide," I continued. "It hurt, but not as much as when Pa took his last breath. He had cancer. Hid that shit until it was too late and refused treatment. Told me he'd had a good life, that I'd made it better, but it was time for him to go because he wanted to see his old lady again. That was ten years ago and when I became the new president." Groaning, I cursed under my breath. "Went a little dark with that information, sorry, darlin'."

"I want to hear everything."

There went my heart again, beating to her rhythm.

"Everythin'? All right, I'm down with that. It just might take a while." Like the rest of our lives together.

Dusty hummed as if she was fine with that too. "Let's see what else I can tell you then. When I was twenty-five — Fuck, I just realized you haven't even made it to twenty-five. Baby, you're young, still have so much ahead of you—"

Her hands tightened around mine. "Don't, please."

She didn't want me to touch on our age difference. Why? Was it because she didn't like it, or she couldn't care less? I hoped and had a feeling it was the latter.

"All right, darlin'." I pressed my lips against the top of her head, something I didn't seem to be able to resist doing, and she tucked herself a little closer. "What I was gonna say was that when I was twenty-five, I crashed my ride for the first time. I wasn't too bad, injury-wise, but my ride was totaled. It crushed me, but Pa surprised me with one he'd been working on for a while. She's still goin' to this day, even after I was run off the road by a rival club a few years later." She flinched at that, her hand gripping me more tightly. "Don't worry though, we got payback on them, and they don't mess with us anymore. One time, I got pulled over by a cop. One who hated our club. He tried to plant some drugs on me. It was lucky the other cop with him was a friend of Death's and pulled him up on it. We've had situations like that all the time. A heap of cops who hate us and only a few who would stand their ground on our side. They don't trust us because there's been situations we've had to involve ourselves in—they knew it, but they couldn't prove we were there at the time and hated us for it, because the… let's say the bad guy wasn't found. We'd taken care of it."

Taking a breath, I rested my hand on her waist, hating I needed to give her this out. "You get that, baby? That we've got cops breathin' down our neck and there's gonna be other shit that comes up with rival clubs or someone who just has the shits with us over somethin'. Just want you to think about that, darlin', make sure the club is where you see yourself in years to come." I kissed her hair and heard her intake of breath as if she was about to talk. I quickly got there first. "Don't answer yet, sugar. Think on it, and we'll talk soon."

Need you to make sure here, this club, me is where you want to be, even when trouble comes.

CHAPTER FIFTEEN

Country

As Lucas expected, the X-ray showed a fracture in Dusty's cheekbone. Since she hadn't eaten, he wanted to do the sedation and procedure right then. Once she was under, I walked from the room with a tightness to my gut. I'd hated seeing her pass the fuck out from the sedatives.

Before I'd headed downstairs, Wreck had already messaged the brothers to get to church. We had shit to discuss. The only ones who'd be missing were Gun since he was assisting Lucas and Saint. He was on guard duty in the basement with a couple of prospects.

By the time I reached the meeting room, the brothers were there. Some stood against the walls, while the main players were seated around a huge-ass table. The only spots left were for Wreck and me. Mine was at the end of the table.

After sitting, I picked up the gavel and hit it down. "Let's get shit out in the air. State, news from the basement?"

"Nothing new from what Wreck told you. But I'll inform the brothers who haven't heard. Dusty was stolen from the clinic, taken to Yano and his gang, but then Duck bought her. If it wasn't for Davina, who had a link to the black market, Duck wouldn't have known anythin' about Dusty. They were going to film Duck killin' her to send to our president."

The brothers roared their hate.

Hitting the gavel again, the brothers quieted. "You all know who Dusty is to us."

"A sister," someone yelled.

"Prez's old lady, if she accepts," Tech added with a smirk.

"She will." I didn't doubt it, but it could just take time for her to agree. Some chuckled. "Now, we need to sort out what we're gonna do with the prisoners before the cops come breathing down our necks after they find out we found Dusty."

"You already got an idea, Prez?" Death asked. He could always read me easily.

"I do. We saw Dusty's boss rock up with Blaze. After

we're done with them, I thought the best way to get rid of them was to offer them to Blaze."

Quake cleared his throat. "For those who don't know, Blaze's clients are people no one wants to fuck with, not even us. The fuckers in the basement will be cut up and body parts sold. I don't know about the rest of you, but I'm down for it. Hell, that was even before seeing Dusty in the state she was in."

"We should have done the same to those other fuckers, but I'm glad I saw the life drain from their eyes personally." Torch grinned. He was right. I wished we had kept the first cunts alive for this plan, but it was good to take their lives ourselves.

"Duck and Davina have been nothing but a pain in our asses. We need to get rid of them as soon as possible, and I agree with Prez; giving them to Blaze for the slow pain they deserve will be good," State said.

"And before the cops show because we'll have to report Dusty as safe," Tech added.

"All in favor to hand them over to Blaze, raise your hands."

It was unanimous.

"Tech, is Blaze still hangin' about?"

Tech snorted. "Yeah. Overheard him tell Henri he doesn't trust us enough to leave Henri alone."

The asshole knew we'd do nothing to Henri since he'd had Dusty's back.

"Right. In a sec I want you to grab him, but first, I

wanna know your thoughts about sending Eve into Davina's room?"

Tech stilled. "Fuck." He ran a hand over his face. "Eve would want in, but it ain't like Davina isn't already in pain." He glanced at Torch.

Torch shrugged as he pulled out a lighter and started playing with it. "When a cunt is a cunt, they deserve some pain."

I couldn't agree more. Which was why I'd be seeing her myself. Nodding at Torch, I turned back to Tech, who said, "I'd prefer to not have Eve in there, but I can't make her decision."

Lifting my chin toward the door, I ordered, "Go talk with her and then get Blaze."

Tech nodded and left the room, closing the door after him.

"While we wait, is there any other order of business?" The sooner I got shit organized, the quicker I could get back to Dusty's side. I prayed everything was going well.

By the time Tech walked back in with Blaze, business shit had been gone over. It was then I realized that if Blaze said no, we'd have to take matters into our own hands like we had Yano and his men. Kill Duck and Davina and quickly get rid of their bodies for a full clean of the club in case the cops showed with some type of botched-up notice that gave them a right to search.

"What's going on?" Blaze asked when he stopped at

the other end of the table, crossing his arms over his chest.

"You got any clients in need of some organs? I have two unwilling subjects."

The smile he showed had a few of the brothers tensing. Torch was the only one who laughed. I'd seen that smile once in our past, and that was before he'd disappeared after his sister had been brutally killed and he'd found the man who'd done it. If Death and I hadn't already been wary of the man back in the day, we would have forced our offered services in helping him in revenge instead of standing back when he'd refused. Though, when he declined, it was for the better, since we knew the man didn't have any type of remorse with the shit he dealt in.

"I'm sure I've got a few in need. Gladly take them off your hands, but I ain't owing any favors for this."

"We don't want one. All we request is that whichever client you pick, they make sure Duck is coherent when the organs are being taken."

Blaze whistled. "Guess you don't look down on people when shit happens to someone you care about."

"Never said I look down on someone, Blaze. If they have a good enough reason for the pain they want to deliver, then so be it. You know what I didn't agree with back in the day." His drug dealing had been a problem for me.

His jaw clenched as he eyed me. "I'll make some calls."

"The sooner, the better, and you might want to get out of here because the cops will have to be notified Dusty was found."

He nodded and made his way out of the room. Tech closed the door after him before he turned back to me. "Eve wants to head down to Davina's room." He didn't seem pleased, and I wasn't sure if I was supposed to regret offering this or not. But she was a grown woman who could make up her own mind.

Hitting the gavel, I stood. "Meeting adjourned." I met Tech at the door and gripped his shoulder. "You sure you're all right with it?"

"She's her own person, and I can't say I don't understand wanting to punch the bitch."

"I'm headin' down. I'll make sure she doesn't go too far."

"Thanks, Prez, but you mind if I come as well?"

"So am I," Quake said, not far away.

"Sure." I nodded. When we got to the basement, we heard the yelling from the end of the hall. Quickening our pace, we swung into the room to see Saint smirking at Eve, who had—fuck me—a plastic bag over Davina's head, restricting her breathing.

Tech sighed. "Knew my sister was on the crazy side, but at least it's to protect those she cares about most."

"Good luck to your future old lady," I muttered.

Tech snorted. "Nah, good luck to whoever her old man will be."

Eve whipped the bag off, and Davina gasped for her breath. Eve slapped the bitch before she turned to us. "I've had my fun." She stalked toward us and handed the bag to Saint. "It'll be a good day when she's not tarnishing the world with her life."

Eve slipped out, and I didn't miss Quake quickly and quietly following her. What was up with that? Not that it was my business.

"I'm gonna have a quick word with Duck before Blaze gets rid of him."

Tech and Saint grinned. "We'll spot you, Prez," Tech offered.

Good. The sooner I delivered my message, the quicker I could shower and be back at Dusty's side. I didn't want her to wake without me there.

HEADING to Dusty's old room, which Lucas had sanitized and turned into a makeshift surgery for the small procedure, I heard clearly Lucas's panicked tone. "Dusty, just stay on the bed. You can't move."

Opening the door, I took in Lucas half lying over Dusty while Gun tried to restrain her feet.

"What the fuck?" I boomed.

They all froze and glanced my way. My gaze settled

on the bandage covering Dusty's cheek. "Country!" she cried and started to struggle again. "No, wait, he told me, *me* to call him Maverick. Gun, Lucas, did you hear me?"

"Get over here and help. She woke up thinking she's invincible from the meds," Gun explained with a smirk.

When I got to her side, I took the hand she had outstretched to me, and she settled. Lucas and Gun looked at her, to me, and back to her. They slowly moved off her.

"Darlin', what trouble are you givin' them?"

"Moi?" She touched her chest with her other hand. "I would never."

Grinning, I bopped her damn cute nose. "Yeah, darlin', you would. You gonna sit still and rest for me?"

She hummed under her breath, glancing off to the side. "You know, I could if…"

"If what?" I asked, my grin growing.

"If you showed me the masterpiece of your cock," she stated, her tone so serious I laughed. I wasn't the only one. At least Lucas tried to hide it behind his hand.

"Baby, maybe when you're not high and we're alone."

She harrumphed and waved her hand at Gun and Lucas. "Begone, peasants." She cackled but quickly sobered. "I was joking. I would never think of you two as peasants. I love you guys. I really do, but I'd like to see Maverick's dick a lot more." Her head tilted to the side a little. "Maverick." She smiled up at me. "I really like your name. Did I say that?"

"You didn't, Dusty."

"I like you saying my name, too, but I love it more when you call me darlin', or sugar, or baby. I just like everything about you. Want to have sex?"

When she started to spread her legs, I pulled them closed with a chuckle. "Darlin', we ain't doin' anythin' right now. You gotta rest."

"Gun?"

"Yes, Dusty?"

"You're super-duper at drawing. Can you draw a picture of Maverick's dick?"

"Fuck no," I clipped.

Gun laughed his ass off. "Don't think the prez likes that idea."

"It's okay," she whispered, staring at Gun. "I'll take a photo of it to keep in my purse. Though, his face is better than his cock. Both give me pleasure—"

Quickly, I covered her mouth with my hand, careful of her injury. "Out, both of you. Lucas, tell me what she needs."

"If you can, get her to rest. It won't help, her talking so much."

"On it. Can I take her back to my room?"

Dusty pulled my hand away. "Ooooh, your room. This special treatment is going to go right to my head, and I'll start to think you care."

"I do, darlin'."

"Nope. Not in the way I want to think you do."

Lucas cleared his throat. "I'll help get her back. She's still on fluids." He nodded toward the IV pole next to the bed as he went around to grab it. I slid my arms under Dusty at her shoulders then knees, and picked her up. Lucas and I maneuvered around each other to get out of the room.

"Dusty, let me know if you need anythin'," Gun called. To me, he muttered, "I'm gonna clear the way in case she tries to party with someone or somethin'." With my nod, he moved off ahead of us.

"Yeah," she said a little breathily, her reply to Gun a little delayed. I glanced down and found her looking up at me. "Hi." She winked.

Chuckling, I shook my head. "Hey, darlin'. You feelin' all right?"

"Oh, I'm feeling *really* good." She winked again as her fingertips walked up my chest. "I have to tell you something."

Lucas groaned. "Can it *please* wait until I'm out of earshot?"

"No," Dusty replied, all serious.

"Baby, it might be better to wait."

She pouted. "But I don't want to. It's only Lucas."

"Who's married to Wreck."

"Oh... I think I'll wait. Wreck might get offended I don't find him as attractive as you."

This woman was going to kill me in mushiness.

"You think I'm hot, baby?"

"The hottest of all hotness. You need a medal for it. Do you know, on the first night, I couldn't take my eyes away from you? I wanted to have your babies, and I still do. I'd like you to plant your delicious seed—"

"Dusty!" Lucas yelled, which was good since I nearly tripped from her words.

She wanted my babies.

Mine.

Even from the damn beginning.

Yeah, I'd been the biggest fucking fool to think Dusty was going to be like all the other club girls who just wanted a fun time with the brothers, myself included.

"Lucas, why are you following Maverick? You're not looking at his ass, are you?"

Snorting at her cute frown, I reassured her, "He's married, remember? He's just helping me get here." I managed to open the door without having to put her down and stepped in.

"Thank God," Lucas groaned.

I'd just placed Dusty on my bed when Lucas shifted the IV closer and bolted from the room, calling over his shoulder, "Make sure she rests. I'll check her in a couple of hours. Good luck."

"This room smells like you. I like your smell."

I had a feeling she liked just about everything about me, but fuck, it was good to hear. Didn't mean after a shit few days that I would play on her drugged-out state and ask what else she liked.

Nah, it was a bad idea.

Wasn't it?

It would be.

But she'd already said so much.

Did a little more matter?

It probably would when she remembered it after the drugs cleared.

"Are we having sex now?" Her hands went under my tee on her body, and she hooked her thumbs into her panties to shimmy them down.

"Hold up there, darlin'."

She stilled. "You don't want me?" Her bottom lip trembled.

"I ain't sayin' that at all. I'd have you in a heartbeat." She smiled. "But it can't be now."

"Why?" she snapped, and hell, I would have laughed if I didn't think she'd hurt herself trying to hit me for it.

Grinning, I slipped onto the bed beside her, curling an arm over Dusty's waist and pulling her close. "Because we're gonna have a rest. I'm dog-tired, darlin'."

"Oh… okay. I could have a sleep with you."

"I'd appreciate it."

"Okay," she whispered, shifting to her side to face me and moving closer to tuck her head under my chin.

Her forehead hit my neck, and she sighed into my skin. "I like this."

"So do I, darlin'." I ran my hand up and down her back, and it didn't take long for her to relax and drift off to sleep or for me to follow.

CHAPTER SIXTEEN

Dusty

ear God, no! Why would Lucas, or Gun for that matter, let me spew everything I had in front of Maverick? Huh, it was still a little strange to use his first name, yet I didn't deny the excitement that rolled through my belly every time I thought of it or used it.

However, I put that all to the side because I hadn't yet finished freaking out over the things I'd said.

Oh shit. I'd even asked Gun to draw a picture of Maverick's dick.

I wanted to bury my head in some sand like an ostrich. I could at least then hide, because even if I tried to disappear, they… the club would come after me.

They'd already done enough, so I couldn't up and leave because of embarrassment.

I was going to have to suck it up and apologize to a few people. But first, I needed pain meds—ones not as strong as the morphine—for the ache in the side of my face.

Rolling to my back, I glanced at the empty spot beside me. Maverick had been there. He'd held me, cared for me, talked to me about his life. There weren't enough words to describe how much that meant to me.

He'd made me feel special. Not just a usual club girl in a rough spot where the brothers pulled together to help. This felt more. Even from the brothers. When they'd found me.... I shook my head, wincing at the fresh throb of pain in my cheek. The only times I'd seen them that angry was when things happened to another brother or one of their partners.

Then again, I could be seeing things. Of course they would be upset to see what I'd been put through. They would have reacted the same if it had happened to another club girl.

Since it had been me, though, I allowed myself to believe their anger and attention was because I was important to them. I deserved some happiness after everything.

My mind quickly took me back to those rooms, to what I could have done better to get myself out of those situations. I knew I'd always wish I'd acted differently, fought more, tried something, but it all came down to remembering I'd done what I could, especially in the harshness of reality.

Only it left me feeling weak.

Tears pricked my eyes. I wanted to blame myself for being put in the situation. Did I make the wrong choice in calling Maverick and not the police? Did I not fight enough? I knew I froze at some points, but—

No. There was nothing I could change. There was nothing I could have done differently.

I wanted to scream, to cry, to rant as the thoughts kept rolling through my mind.

Shut up, shut up, shut up.

Sniffing, I wiped at my face, maneuvering around the bandage, just before the door opened and Maverick walked in holding a tray.

"Shit, you're awake. I wanted to be here, sorry."

"Um, it's fine." I took a quick wipe at my face when he turned to shut the door again. Wincing, I slowly sat up as he made his way over to the bed. With a smile, he deposited the tray on my lap and then walked around the bed to sit beside me.

Maverick nodded toward the tray. "Pain meds on there, darlin'. Lucas said you might need some."

"Thank you."

"Nothin' to it, Dusty." He settled back against the headboard and grabbed the extra coffee off the tray as I moved mine to the bedside table. Left on the tray was a bowl of oatmeal. Since it was soft, I wouldn't have to chew too much. Such thought into what would be easy for me to eat sent a thrill of warmth into my chest.

However, I couldn't eat, not with the sudden wave of nerves that hit me. I'd asked this man, this smoking-hot man, to plant his seed in me, *and* it was in front of Lucas.

Since he was sitting on the side where I had my good eye, I peeked his way and caught his smirk before he took a sip of his coffee.

"You good, darlin'?"

"Yep." I popped the *p*.

"You gotta be hungry."

Unable to take it anymore, I blurted, "I'm so sorry I said the stuff I did. I promise I'm not sneakily trying to trap you into marriage and a baby. I'm not like that. I said some things I shouldn't have and—"

"Dusty?"

Closing my mouth, I dropped my gaze from the wall to the bed. "Yes?"

"It's fine, sugar. I didn't mind at all."

Snorting, I shook my head. "You should. I can't believe what I said."

"Baby, don't stress. It's all good."

"Are you sure? I can go back to my room. Well, another one since the X-ray—"

"Dusty."

I gripped the bedding. "Yes?"

Softly, he said, "You ain't goin' anywhere."

My heart stumbled in my chest.

"You okay with that?" he added.

Well, I did say I want to have your babies, and I only half didn't mean it. "Ah, sure."

He hummed and took another sip of his coffee.

Blowing out a gentle breath, I asked, "Do we need to talk about what I said? I don't want you scared I'm going to put holes in your condoms or anything."

He chuckled. "Jesus, Dusty. I know you'd never do that." He shook his head. "Just forget it, yeah?"

"Really?"

"Yes, darlin'."

"Okay, as long as you're sure."

His brow rose as he smirked, and his gaze lit with humor. "Baby" was all he said.

Well... all right. If he preferred to leave it, I guess I could. Picking up the meds, I took a gulp of coffee and swallowed them down. I placed my coffee back down and grabbed the bowl.

Testing the spoonful on my lip, I took a mouthful.

"Let me know if you want a picture of my cock."

The oatmeal flew across the bed as I coughed it out, my face heating. I cringed at the bigger movement pulling at my cheek.

"Fuck, sorry, darlin', I didn't mean to make it hurt."

Licking the oatmeal off my lips, I blurted, "I don't mind a bit of pain." Gasping, I quickly told him, "I didn't mean it *that* way," when he started chuckling.

I grabbed a napkin from the tray, but Maverick took it from my hand. "I'll get it. You eat."

Maybe it was best I did, so I kept my mouth shut.

After Maverick cleaned and got rid of the napkin in the bathroom bin, he slid back on the bed next to me with a warm smile. Which I returned and nearly dribbled oatmeal out. I sucked that sucker back in quickly.

Swallowing, I stirred the oatmeal around. "Ah, I didn't mean to say that about your... you know, and ask Gun to draw it."

Another laugh fell from his mouth. "Know that, darlin', but you know he'll give me shit in front of the brothers about it."

That was what I was afraid of.

"I'll talk to him. Tell him not to."

He grinned. "Won't bother me, Dusty. It was funny. Glad you like the sight of my dick that much."

Again, my face burned. "Oh my God," I groaned. "Can we, um, not talk about that one either?"

"Sure, baby." His smirk said otherwise, which was swept away with whatever thought took over.

"Maverick, are you okay?" I took another spoonful of oatmeal but then placed the bowl back on the tray.

"Darlin', it's me who should be askin' that."

"I'm..." He shot me a look, and I knew if I lied, he wouldn't appreciate it. "It'll take time, but I'll get there. Do you think, um, would my parents know I was missing?"

"We called the cops after we'd been through the vet clinic. No doubt they would have reached out to your parents."

"Shit. I should call them."

"I'll grab your phone soon. The cops have only contacted Henri once since you've been gone. Maybe if they pulled their thumbs outta their asses, they would have found more answers." By the way he was now white-knuckling his coffee cup, Maverick was pissed at the police. His phone rang, and I caught Death's name light up the screen. Maverick answered, "Yeah, brother?" His upper lips raised in a silent snarl at the door. "Get Lucas in here, and we'll be down in a sec." When he hung up, he turned to me. "Speakin' of cops, they're here."

My stomach rolled. "What do I do? What do I say?"

Maverick put his cup down and grabbed my hand. "Relax, darlin'. All you gotta say is that the clinic got broken into for drugs, you got taken when they found you, but they let you go, threw you outta a van when their boss said to get rid of you. You don't know what they look like or what the van is. You walked from Jefferson Street to here. From Jefferson Street to the compound, there aren't any cameras, so they can't prove you're lying."

Nodding, I repeated it in my mind as Maverick grabbed the tray off my lap and placed it at the end of the bed after he stood.

"Do I need to change?"

"No, baby. Stay in that. You haven't been back long. We patched you up before calling the cops."

"Okay, all right. I can do this."

A knock sounded, and my throat closed. Lucas stuck his head in before he moved into the room. "I'll take the needle out." His gentle nature shone when he slid the needle out without any pain attached. He placed a Band-Aid over it and frowned. "Maybe slip a long sleeve under the tee, so they don't see it. The bandage on the face can be explained." He glanced to Maverick.

"Dusty knows what to say."

"All right." Lucas nodded. He gripped my hand and squeezed. "You've got this."

"Thanks, Lucas."

He waved off my thanks as he moved out the room and Maverick stepped out of the walk-in-robe with a Henley. He helped me remove his tee and put the Henley on before slipping his tee back over my head. I pushed my arms into the sleeves and glanced up at Maverick.

He used the backs of his fingers to slightly brush over my uninjured cheek. "You'll be fine. I'll be right at your side, darlin'."

"Okay." I held out my hand to him, and with a gentle smile, he took it. Maverick kept my gaze when he brought my hand up to kiss the back of it.

He held my hand until we got to the stairs, where he

slipped his arm around my waist to help me down them. Thankfully the pain meds were already doing their job and taking the sharper pain down to a dull ache.

When we entered the common room, Maverick took my hand again and slowly led me over to the couch area while I took in the five officers looking around the area until they spotted us. "Dusty'll talk to you over here." Maverick helped lower me down to the couch and then sat beside me, curling an arm along the back of the couch and around my shoulders.

The only others in the room were Death, State, Quake, and Tech. Quake tipped his chin up my way as the cops, all frowning, made their way over. Two sat on the opposite couch while the other three stood behind it. One was a woman who wouldn't quit looking at Maverick like he was candy she wanted to try.

The officer on the left on the couch, who was a bit older, cleared his throat. "Miss Reyes, my name's Officer Plank, and I'll be honest, we're actually surprised to see you here. We came to question some of the people who live here after we found out you... uh, worked here."

"I don't work here. I work at the vet clinic and at Flourished Florist."

"So, you just *live* here?"

"Here and at my parents'."

"Yes, your parents who knew nothing of this residence when I informed them earlier."

"My parents and I aren't close. What does any of this have to do with what happened to me?"

He smiled, but it didn't reach his eyes, which kept flicking to Maverick all the time. "Just trying to figure things out."

"Tell us what happened at the clinic," the other man, who seemed about thirty, asked from beside Officer Plank. "Sorry, I'm Officer Jones."

"On the way to the vet clinic, I got a flat tire outside the factory, which is just down the road. I walked the rest of the way and started my normal routine when I heard people outside the front door breaking in."

"Had you ever seen them before?"

"No. Well, I did call my employer previously when I noticed a car watching the place."

He nodded. "Your employer said the same. What did you do when you heard them?" He flicked a page of his notebook. "It says you made one phone call, and that was to Maverick Evans."

"I panicked. I hid in a room, knowing that if I went out the back, the dogs would have given me away. Before I realized I should have called the cops, I was already on the phone to Maverick."

"Why him? Does it have anything to do with you being a club girl and being his favorite?" Officer Plank smirked.

Maverick shifted, and I knew he was about to blow a gasket. I quickly placed my hand on his thigh and ran it up and down before saying, "My being a club girl has nothing to do with the situation, and if you bring it up again, I'll file for harassment." Leaning forward a little, I asked, "Don't you want to know why my face is busted up instead of judging me and my living situation?"

Plank's smirk dropped right off. Officer Jones shot him a look. "Please, continue, Miss Reyes."

Sighing, I rested back against the couch, closer to Maverick that time, glaring at the woman officer who glanced away. I informed them of everything Maverick said to. How I was blindfolded and didn't see who they were or where they took me. "They knocked me out, and when I woke, I was in a car—a van, I think, since all I could feel under me was metal flooring. I didn't know how long I was out for, but they kept driving until one of them got a phone call. As soon as their boss, whoever that was, told them to get rid of me, they drove for some time longer before opening the door while the van was still moving and pushing me from it." I waved at my face. "It's how this happened. I pulled the blindfold off, noted it was a new day and that I was on Jefferson Street, so I walked my way here, knowing I would be safe within the compound."

"And how long ago was that?" Plank asked while Jones murmured something to one of the officers, who nodded and shifted away to make a phone call.

"About an hour ago," Maverick supplied. "We got

her injuries looked at and were about to call you guys before you showed."

"Convenient." Plank shook his head.

"Miss Reyes, is there anything you could tell me about the men? Did you see anything at all, even the smallest glimpse? Or anything about their voices."

"No, sorry. They didn't have any accents, if that's what you mean."

Jones sighed. "All right, that's okay."

"Maverick, or should I call you Country?" Plank asked.

"Actually, you can call me Mr. Evans."

Plank's jaw clenched. "Fine. Mr. Evans. Do you know a Blaze McCoy?"

"I do, and you'd know that from research since we went to the same high school."

"Can you tell us when the last time was you saw him?"

A throat cleared. We all looked toward the entry-way. "No need to pester someone else about me, Prick. I'm right here." Who was this guy, and why was he here?

"It's Plank."

Blaze cocked a brow. "That's what I said."

"What are you doing here, McCoy?" Plank demanded.

"He's here with me." Henri stepped out from behind Blaze's tall and wide form to gently lean into Blaze's side. "Blaze and I are lovers, and I'm sure you can guess why I'm here."

Blaze rolled his eyes but curled his arm around Henri's waist.

What in the what and who?

"Mr. Duolle. I didn't realize you and Miss Reyes were that close," Jones said while writing in his notepad.

"Of course we are. I told Officer Plant I would like to know anything new on Dusty's case because she and I had become close friends."

Jones glanced to Plank, who looked irritated from the way his face glowed red. I expected since Henri got his name wrong as well.

"Dusty's given her statement of the event. Unless there's anythin' else, I'm gonna ask you all to leave so she can get some rest."

Jones stood, but Plank didn't. "I have another question."

"Plank, not now," Jones clipped, which had Plank glaring up at him. Obviously, he didn't like being told what to do by a younger guy. "Harred?" he called.

"No video surveillance in or around Jefferson Street."

Plank scoffed as he stood. "Funny how that is."

"Thank you for your time, Miss Reyes." Jones handed me a card. "Please contact me if you have anything else to add."

"I will."

Jones tucked his notepad into his pocket. "I'm presuming this is where you'll be staying if we have any other questions?"

"Yes," I replied with a nod.

Jones eyed us one last time before Death stepped forward and said, "I'll show you all out." Plank got in one last glower our way before he followed the rest out.

Henri was in my space as soon as the door closed, kneeling on the floor in front of me and taking my hand. "My dear, how are you feeling?"

"I'm okay, Henri." Blaze grunted from where he stood behind Henri. "Who is that?" I muttered to my boss.

Henri rolled his eyes. "Just Blaze. Don't worry about him. Tell me if there's anything I can do?"

"Really, there's nothing." I smiled softly.

"Well, you will be having the week off, *with* pay, boss's orders."

"Henri—"

His hand shot up. "Non, boss's orders, and you know how grumpy I can get when I'm not listened to. If you need more than a week, you shall have it."

My smile grew. "I won't."

He harrumphed and turned to Maverick. "You'll let me know if she needs it, oui?"

"Yeah, Henri, I will."

"Merci. Now, I will take my leave and let you rest."

He stood, leaned in, and kissed my good cheek. "I'll come back another day, and we'll gossip."

A laugh escaped me. "All right." On a whisper, I added, "And I want to know all about Blaze."

He pulled back, nodded, and faced Blaze. "Let us leave."

Blaze grunted, but he looked to Maverick. "That thing is done."

Maverick tipped his chin up. "Good."

When they left, I glanced up at the man beside me. "What thing? Do you really know Blaze from high school? Was what Henri said real? Are they lovers?"

"Darlin'." He grinned. "Find out the gossip from Henri when he comes back. The rest you don't need to worry about, but I will tell you that Blaze and I did go to the same high school." He dipped, pressing his lips to my temple. "You did well, baby."

"Fuck yeah, she did." Tech chuckled.

"You made Plank your bitch. Good work, sister." Quake nodded, smiling wide.

Screwing up my nose, I shrugged slightly. "He was an ass."

The men around me chuckled. Maverick adjusted me, so I wasn't leaning into him before he stood. "Time for bed again, darlin'. Quake, make some soup, yeah?"

"You got it, Prez."

"Don't burn down my kitchen," I called just as Maverick picked me up in his arms.

Quake snorted. "I'll try not to."

I sighed into Maverick's hold as he carried me, thinking about the difference between having Maverick at my side and my family supporting me. As that's what this MC was to me.

Shit, that reminded me I still had to call my parents.

CHAPTER SEVENTEEN

Dusty

*W*hen we reached the bedroom, Maverick gave me time to call my parents in private from my phone he'd pulled from his back pocket. I didn't know when he got it. Not that it mattered. What I worried about now was what would be best to tell my parents. Thanks to the police, they now knew I was a club girl at the Diamond MC.

I waited for the shame to uncurl, but it never did. There was no room to feel ashamed, not when the men I surrounded myself with were good men. I was never treated badly or forced. Instead, I was taken care of. Needed. Wanted.

Sighing, I pressed on Dad's name in my contact list.

It only got one ring in before he answered, "Dusty. Dear God, where are you? Are you all right?"

"I'm okay, Dad."

"Are you at… that place?"

"If you mean the Diamond MC compound, then yes, that's where I am."

"Your mother and I will be there shortly."

"Dad, I'm really tired. Can we make it later?"

He grumbled something. "We'll be there before dinner."

"Okay. See you then." When I hung up, I gripped my cell to my chest. My parents were coming to the compound. I realized too late it would have been better to meet them someplace. I expected they'd arrive and judge everything and everyone.

The door opened, and Maverick stood in it with another tray. "Didn't hear any voices, figured it was all right to come in." He walked my way and placed the tray on my lap after I scooted back to lean against the headboard.

"I could get used to this service," I teased, but really, the attention was going to my head and putting bad ideas in my mind, like what it would be like to be Maverick's.

Maverick grinned as he walked back around the bed. I didn't miss his gaze on my phone. "Everythin' go okay?"

"I probably should have checked with you first, but

my parents wanted to come here this afternoon, just before dinner. Is that okay?"

He sat and leaned back. "No need to check with me, darlin'. You can do anythin'. Later I'll let the brothers at the gate know we'll be expecting them." He grabbed a plate of toasted sandwiches and nodded toward the soup. "Eat while it's warm. It ain't anythin' like you'd cook, but it's edible. I checked."

He'd checked.

Knowing he had warmed my lower belly.

Taking up the bowl, I took a few spoonfuls and eyed his room. A television was mounted in the corner, and beside the bed was a bar fridge. Along with a chair and the bedside tables, it was all the room consisted of. I liked it. Even his comforter, which was a light gray, suited the room and Maverick.

I still couldn't get over the fact he'd asked me to call him Maverick. It made me dare to hope it meant something to him as much as it did me. That hope was dangerous.

Maverick placed his plate on the bedside table and stood. He went to the little fridge and grabbed a couple of bottles of water. When he sat, he put one on the tray for me.

"Thanks."

"Darlin'."

"Yes?"

"You said to the cop you and your 'rents aren't close. Can I ask why?"

As I sorted out my answer in my head, I finished off the soup and dropped the bowl on the tray. "It's not that we don't get along. More, we don't really know each other. I'm their background noise. They're driven by work and money, and at a young age, I learned to take care of myself, because... well, to be honest, I felt it would be better to do things myself than receive their looks of annoyance when I asked something."

"Fuck, baby, that would have been hard. No wonder you were lookin' to spice up your life when you joined here."

Laughter bumbled out. "Exactly. I've never had many friends, as I always had my nose stuck in a book or the yard planting flowers or cooking."

"You got a family now, darlin'. You know that, right?" He took the tray from my lap after passing me the bottle of water, which I put on the bedside table. Butterflies in my belly took off in flight.

"I do. I really love it here."

He turned toward me and studied my face. "You're serious," he stated.

"Completely. I love cooking in the kitchen, working in the yard out back, which was a disaster before I got to it."

"Shit, that was you. Baby, out back looks like a damn oasis."

I smiled proudly, which pulled a little, but I didn't care. "It does."

"You got skills, woman. You're important here. Need you to know that."

Feeling suddenly shy, I glanced down at the sheet covering my legs. "I don't know if I can agree with that. But thank you. Being here has always brought a smile to my face whenever I woke up."

"Fuck, darlin', you're killin' me."

Lifting my gaze, I watched him scrub a hand over his face. "How?"

He shook his head, his gaze on my hand fisting the sheet. Reaching out, he unhooked my fingers and joined his to mine. "Do you think your 'rents are gonna cause an issue this afternoon?"

He completely ignored my question, and I wasn't sure if I wanted to press it.

"I doubt it. They'll pop in, check on me, and leave. Besides, I'm not in the mood to see them really."

I watched as his thumb ran over the back of my hand. He grunted. "Why's that?"

"Because, before what happened, I found out my mom isn't my real mother."

"Shit, Dusty, how'd you find out?"

"I overheard her and her girlfriend talking." My stomach tightened. I didn't want to think about the lies. "Anyway, do you mind if I had a nap? I'd like to shower before my parents arrive." Did I still call them my parents when she wasn't my mother? Yet, the image of her teaching me math popped into my mind. She may have been the colder one toward me, but she had been there.

"Do anythin' you want, sugar." My gaze swept up to him when he gently tucked some hair behind my ear. "I'm gonna rest here with you for a little before I have to catch up on things with the business."

"You don't have to stay—"

"I'm stayin'."

"I, ah, I'm just going to the bathroom quickly. Be back." He tipped his chin up to me and let go of my hand. I scooted out of bed and walked to the bathroom, glancing back to see Maverick already lying flat with an arm thrown across his eyes. His tee was pulled up, skin peeking out.

I knew what that skin tasted like.

God, why was I thinking of that now when I couldn't do anything about the arousal suddenly running through me? After I'd finished in the bathroom, I opened the door to see Maverick in the same place as before.

When I slipped back under the sheet, which he lay on, I rested on my side to face him. Thankfully it was my better side, though my other cheek still throbbed.

It was wrong to keep watching him. Was he asleep? Was he awake and waiting to see what I would do? I knew he wouldn't expect anything sexual from me, but I did want to touch him in some way.

With a slow, tired blink, I wiggled closer, and with my heart in my throat, I reached out to rest my hand on his chest. A sigh fell from his mouth as he rolled my way. Taking my hand in both of his, he held it between us, close to his heart. I felt his lips press against the top of my head. "Rest, darlin'," he ordered, but I was already drifting off with a small content smile on my lips.

FROM WHERE I sat at a table, I could easily see when someone walked in the door. My hands shook, and I didn't understand the uneasy grip on my stomach. Though, no matter what my parents said, I would stand up for my real family.

Glancing across the room, my gaze landed on Maverick. He was busy talking to State and Death, but it was as if he felt my stare, and our eyes locked. He cocked his head to the side. I took it as a question, asking if I was okay. I sent him a smile, and he tipped his chin my way.

"It's cute," Courtney said.

"What?" Eve snapped.

"Dusty and Country."

A noise, half choke, half laugh tumbled from my

mouth. "What are you talking about?"

"Amour, it is clear to see you two have a connection." Henri nodded to himself as he watched Blaze
walk from the room. No doubt he was heading down
the hall to Tech's room. Henri told me Blaze and Tech
had bonded over computers and how disgusting all
their boring talk was.

"There is nothing between Country and me. Can we
get back to Blaze and you?"

"Non," Henri said simply. "I am not in the mood to
speak of that buffoon."

Eve snorted. "Fair enough. You know what I heard?"

"What?" Courtney asked.

"How Country threw a chair across the room when
Tech couldn't find where Dusty was."

"Ooh-la-la, this is juicy." Henri grinned and pointed
at me. "And you still deny something between you two.
It is clear as the sun is shining through the window."

Blood rushed to my head, and I was too busy trying
to breathe normally to answer.

I looked back to Maverick as he laughed at
something.

He'd acted like that for me?

"He's... he asked me to call him Maverick."

Henri gasped, Courtney's eyes widened, and Eve
laughed as she hit the table with a fist. "You two might
as well set up a wedding date. Tell her, Court."

Courtney nodded. "It's true. No brother will allow a

woman to call him by his given name unless they're serious about you. Dominic didn't tell me to use his real name until after our second date."

Did that mean Maverick was serious about me?

Me?

"I... I don't know what to think or say."

They all cackled. Henri patted my hand. "It's all right, amour. Let the knowledge of Country wanting you sink in. But wait until you're healed to jump his bones. We don't want you hurting something else."

"Henri," I clipped.

He waved me off, but my attention swung to the door when I heard it open. Saint stepped in first and then my parents. Both were dressed in suits, only Mom's was a skirt one. Their indifferent gazes locked on mine as they followed Saint over to the table.

A warm hand cupped the back of my neck. Maverick had walked over to offer his support. My heart zigzagged in my chest.

Dad's expression cracked first, and worry pinched his brows together. "Dusty, what happened?" He flicked a look to Maverick and back down to me.

The room was too quiet. There weren't many of us around, but enough to have made some noise. "Take a seat," I offered as Eve and Courtney moved down the long table. My parents sat opposite me, and I noticed their distance even more than before. "I was kidnapped from the vet clinic and held blindfolded until their boss got rid of me." I pointed to my cheek. "They threw me out of a moving van. I walked here, got patched up, and spoke to the police about it all."

"Do you know who they were? Have the police found them? Will you still be in danger? Why did they take you?" Dad asked with worry in his tone.

Maverick's hand massaged my neck. It helped settle me. "They won't come back. They were only after the drugs and took me in a panic."

"You shouldn't have been working at the clinic so late." Dad frowned.

"I liked working there because of the animals, and the late hours don't bother me."

His jaw clenched. "It's not like you need the money. We give you an allowance."

Closing my eyes, I shook my head slightly. "I gave you your bank card back. I haven't used your money for years because I am my own independent woman. What you've both taught me to be." I always wanted to stand on my own two feet rather than rely on them for anything. In all honesty, they never made me feel like a part of the family and I never wanted to be indebted to them.

"An independent woman wouldn't take a job cleaning a vet clinic in the middle of the night," Mom snapped. "This whole episode has caused us nothing but grief, Dusty. You should have been smarter and not had that job or been taken in the first place."

"Excuse fucking me," Eve bit out.

"Eve, it's fine."

Mom glanced down at Eve and screwed her nose up. "Yes, let's speak of this place. To learn your daughter has taken up with the likes of these people was not only a shock but distasteful. If you have anything here, Dusty, go and retrieve it. You'll be coming home with us."

"Dusty?" Maverick asked, his tone rough and dangerous.

Mom tipped her head back to look at him. "Who are you exactly?"

"Ain't any of your business unless Dusty says it is."

Mom laughed. "Oh, wonderful. You hang about men who can't even speak properly."

"Stop it," I barked.

"Dusty, we're worried about you. Of course we'll want you to come home," Dad tried, using his soft, pleasing tone to get what he wanted.

It wouldn't work, though.

I didn't even bother looking at him. I kept my hard glare on her. "How dare you come in here thinking you can speak about *my* family as you have and try to order me around." I threw out a hand. "This place, these amazing people, have been more of a family to me in two years than either of you have in my whole damn life."

Mom scoffed and rolled her eyes. "Yes, and we know

why that is."

"You—"

I cut Eve off with a look. "Do you know how many men I've slept with since being here for two years?"

"We don't need to hear this," Dad said, his face heating.

"*One man*. Only one, and that was twice in the last two years. I love being here, and these men allow me to make my own choices, give me freedom to be myself. They never expected anything from me. You do not get to judge anyone in here." Taking a shuddering breath, I added, "And I'm not leaving. This is *my* home, *my* family. I'll stay where I'm not a burden, where I'm wanted and cared for."

"Dusty," Dad said, his voice almost broken. Tears filled his eyes.

"You're being difficult, Dusty. Get your things now." Mom stood, crossing her arms over her chest.

"Did you tell Dad I know that you're not my real mother? Yeah, I overheard that," I added at her shocked look, "and how you're sleeping with Charlie? How I know your marriage is a scam? All for business. How Dad has a side woman as well? Do not stand there all prim and proper and expect respect from me or have me listen to you and your orders. I'm not leaving, and that is final."

Maverick's hands settled on my shoulders. "You can both go now."

"Liam, do something," Mom ordered. Though could I really continue calling her Mom? More to the point, did I want to?

Dad blinked up at his wife. "Dusty knows?"

Mom, no, Rebecca, rolled her eyes. "You've coddled her too much. She would have found out eventually."

"Coddle?" I laughed. "I've been doing everything on my own since I was seven years old because you two were too busy working."

Dad blanched. "I... I... I'm sorry, Dusty."

My heart clenched. "I'm not sure if it's too little too late right now, Dad."

"I can make this up to you. I can be better. I thought you were fine with being alone. I thought you were always good at entertaining yourself."

Ice stabbed through my veins. "I can entertain myself, and I enjoy my own company, Dad." I huffed, looking away and catching Henri giving me a sad smile. "Still, I would have given anything to have you take a night off to spend time with me. To get to know me."

He nodded over and over until he said, "I'll change. I will."

"Why?" I asked. I didn't understand why he looked and sounded desperate to keep me in his life.

"Because you're my daughter."

"How about we leave it for now, come back to this another day? Dusty's still recovering." Maverick ran his hands up and down my shoulders and upper arms.

"Yes, of course, anything," Dad said.

"Don't expect me to fold as your father has." Rebecca looked down her nose at me.

"I would never." I glanced back to Dad. "I'll have to come by the house at some point to get my things."

"Just call me, anytime, and I'll make sure I'm there… or if you don't want me to be, I'll go."

Rebecca scoffed. "Really, Liam, you're like a whimpering fool begging for a small amount of attention."

Dad landed a scowl on her just before he blurted, "It happens when you have a heart, Rebecca, and one day Charlotte will see beyond your money to the coldness inside."

Rebecca's face went bright red. "I'll wait in the car." She turned and left without saying anything more, which was probably for the best.

Dad sighed and ran a hand over the back of his neck. "Sorry… about so much." His sad eyes lifted from the table to mine.

"We'll talk soon, Dad."

"Okay." He nodded and flicked his gaze up to Maverick. It stayed, and my heart dropped like lead to my feet when he asked, "Can I ask who you are to my daughter?"

"Dad, that—"

"I'm hers."

Gasps—my own included—as well as chuckles sounded.

"Hers?" Dad muttered, brows pinched. Meanwhile, I stilled and gaped, with nothing but the words ringing around in my mind.

I'm hers.

That could mean anything.

"He means they're dating, Mr. Reyes," Courtney supplied, and Maverick didn't correct her.

My head whipped her way, and I winced, touching my cheek. She sat beside a grinning Henri. Eve also had a happy gleam in her eyes.

Dad cleared his throat. "Right. Well..." His hand went out to Maverick. "It's good to meet you. I'm Liam."

"Country."

Dad's head jerked back. "Country."

"Yeah, president of the Diamond MC."

"Oh, well, okay." He glanced back down at me, and I quickly closed my mouth and formed a smile, hoping I didn't look as shocked as I felt. "We'll speak soon?"

Clearing my throat, I nodded. "We will." Dad ran his gaze over my face one more time before he nodded and started for the door.

Now I had to work out what I was supposed to do after Maverick threw "I'm hers" into the room like it was normal.

CHAPTER EIGHTEEN

Country

Fucking hell. I was the biggest dickhead on the planet. I just hurled that out there in front of everyone, but more importantly, in front of Dusty. Who I hadn't even talked to about something more between us. Still, I couldn't stop the words coming out when her dad asked. I'd needed him to know that I'd be the one to fuck him up if he screwed with my woman.

I still couldn't believe she'd been seven years of age and taking care of herself. How in the fuck had she turned out as she had? I'd have been bitter as fuck. She was the opposite.

Saint walked her dad out, and I waited until the door closed. "Everyone scatter," I ordered. State snorted.

Death smirked, but he ducked his head to hide the action. The women flat-out grinned, as did Henri. But at least they all scattered.

I grabbed the chair beside Dusty. Her cheeks pinked, and she peeked a glance at me but quickly turned away.

"Darlin', look at me."

She turned her face my way and stared at my chin. Grabbing her legs, I gently pulled her around to tuck both legs between mine and rested my hands on her thighs. Christ, there hadn't been a jumble of nerves messing up my gut like this for decades.

"Gotta talk to you about somethin'."

"Okay," she breathed.

"Know what you said to Davina and that other woman when they were saying shit about me and the brothers."

Her mouth popped open, then she swallowed. "You do?"

"Yeah, baby. I hafta say, we appreciate the way you had our backs. But even before knowin' that, we've seen that you're somethin' special." She sucked her lips between her teeth. "The brothers look at you as a sister. Like they do Courtney. They do... but I don't." Tears welled in her eyes. Hell, was I fucking this up already? "I was gonna wait a few weeks before I brought this up, but darlin', I can't. Because if I did, I'd just be wastin' more time and I reckon we've wasted enough."

"Maverick," she whispered, voice thick with emotions, and I damn prayed they were good ones.

Leaning in, I cupped the side of her face. "Not sure where you see your future, darlin', but for me, it's got you in it. Need you to know I was wantin' somethin' to start between us that'll lead to you bein' my old lady. I gotta make sure you understand what that means, though, because you'll be tying yourself to me, someone's who's a fuckload older than you, to this life we have here, the club, but also away from here. Where I work, what I do, and where you're gonna live."

Her lips popped out of their grip as her brows shot up. "I'm going to live here, right?"

Nodding, I cupped her other cheek and held her gaze. "Yeah, you are, but when I don't stay here, I want you at my side at my house."

"You have a house?"

An abrupt chuckle left me. "Yeah, I have a house."

"I didn't know."

"You thought I slept here all the time?"

She shrugged. "I just presumed. But to get back on track and so I'm not imagining anything... are you saying you want to date me?"

Since I couldn't resist, I threaded my fingers through her hair and pressed my lips to the corner of her mouth. "We'll start there, but eventually, I'm gonna marry you, Dusty."

"Oh," she panted out.

Pulling back, I saw the tears in her eyes again, but they didn't fall. "Punch me if I'm being too fast and fuckin'—"

Her hands gripped my tee, and she tugged me up with her as she stood to wrap her arms around my waist. I watched as she licked her lips, then said, "You want me, even after I asked you to plant your seed in me?"

Grinning, I brushed my nose softly against hers. "I've always wanted you. It just took me a fuckin' long time to get my thumb outta my ass and act on it. I've fucked up, baby. But you gotta know there hasn't been anyone since the last time we were together."

"Davina said as much. I… I tried to stop myself from caring about you, but I couldn't. You're all I see, all I feel, and all I want back."

"Fuck, baby." I groaned, dropping another soft kiss to the corner of her mouth.

"I-I'm sorry I'm injured—"

"Never apologize for somethin' that ain't your fault. We know we got somethin' growin' between us. That's all that matters. The physical stuff can come later, because, Dusty, I ain't willin' to set back your healin'. We can wait a little longer for that while we learn about each other more." Gently, I tugged on her hair, and she gave me more of her face. "But don't expect me to resist from holdin' you, sugar. Now I know you want my hands on you, and I won't be able to resist." I slid my other hand down to just above her ass, then back up. "It means I can do this more freely too," I uttered against her temple before kissing her there.

"Maverick?"

"Yeah, darlin'?" I asked, kissing her cheek, jaw, and neck.

"I have to be honest here."

Pulling back, I asked, "What about?"

"Well, I need you to know that I'm going to be suffering while healing. It's been a long time since our last time, and I'm looking forward to our next already."

Smirking, I cocked a brow. "You'll be suffering?"

"Immensely."

Chuckling, I shook my head a little. "Darlin', I'll be right there with you." She smiled, and suddenly a blush hit her cheeks. "Baby, you gotta tell me what just ran through your mind."

The blush deepened, spreading down her neck. "Nothing," she said too quickly, before she placed her forehead against my chest. "I'm just really happy. After everything, how can I be this happy?"

Fucking Christ, my chest expanded as my heart filled with emotion she put in there. "Glad you're happy, Dusty," I whispered, kissing her hair, "because I am too."

Finally. Fucking finally, Dusty and I were starting out along the road where we were meant to be.

SOMETIME LATER, I glanced across the room and found my woman already looking my way. I ran my gaze over her, trying to read if she was okay. Her smile tugged at my heart. I tipped my chin her way, silently asking if she was all right, even though it was her friends surrounding her. When she nodded, I relaxed a little more. Yet I didn't think the tension would completely leave me until she was healed. I hated seeing her marred face, her damaged wrist, or the cuts and bruises. Each time I looked, they reminded me of the hell she'd been through.

My attention wandered to the people around her. When it landed on Blaze, who sat at the end of the table with his eyes on Henri, my gaze narrowed. Did he seriously still think Henri was at risk here around us? Though the way he watched Henri, I didn't think that was the case. It fucking annoyed me he was still about, but he'd done us a favor, even if it came through Henri prompting him.

"Prez," Tech called, stopping beside the table I sat at with Death, Saint, and Gun. "Got a text."

Confusion had my brows dropping. "And?"

He handed me the phone.

Unknown number: **The police will be showing tomorrow with a warrant. They believe the club is**

involved in the disappearance of Yano Levin and Donald Spring.

"Do you know who sent it?" I asked Tech as I handed the phone to Death.

"Wanted to show you first, but I'm gonna grab Blaze and see what we can find."

Death snorted. "Let them come. We have nothing to hide."

"We don't have anythin' now." I smirked. Gun handed the phone to Tech after reading it. I nodded Blaze's way. "Take him and see what you find."

"Will do, Prez."

I watched Tech stop at Blaze's side and utter something before showing him the phone. I caught the interest in Blaze's gaze before he stood and followed Tech down to his room.

"Saint, send word out to the brothers. Gun, get rid of any weapons lying around. Come tomorrow, this compound will be spick-and-span. Death, need you to oversee it, because I'm gonna be busy with my woman."

"No problem, Prez." Death took a gulp of his beer. "From the looks she's been givin' you, I'm guessin' the talk went well."

"Surprised it took you this long to ask."

"Don't usually involve myself in others' private business—"

Saint let out an abrupt laugh. "Bullshit."

Death glared at him. "Maybe I do, but on *this* instance, I didn't because those two needed to get their own heads and hearts together. Just needed to check you two finally have manned the hell up, so you're not an ass whenever you see her around another single brother."

Rolling my eyes, I shook my head. "I was never an ass, and you really think you should talk to me like that?"

Death snorted but said nothing. Yeah, he knew he was one of the few who could say whatever the fuck he wanted to me.

"She's mine now, since she's agreed."

Death grinned. "Thank fuck for that."

"Congrats, Prez." Saint nodded. "Though, from the way you two look at each other, I'm guessin' everyone will have it figured out."

I grunted. "Good."

"She's a good woman," Gun said, playing with the bottle of beer in his hand.

"I know."

"Not one to fuck over." He looked up at me then.

My jaw clenched. "You tryin' to tell me somethin'?"

"You'll always have my respect, Prez. But I gotta tell you, that woman, your woman, has been half in love with you for a fuckin' long time. I reckon it'd break her if this shit ain't serious."

"Never said I wasn't serious, Gun."

"He doesn't mean anythin' by it, Country," Saint tried for his man.

I held my hand up to him and leaned toward Gun. "Understand you want to have her back, Gun. I appreciate it. But don't fuckin' question me and how serious I am about my woman."

"Prez," Saint started, until Gun reached over and ran his hand up and down Saint's thigh.

"Won't happen again, Prez," Gun answered.

Standing, I ordered, "Go do the shit I asked." When they nodded, I turned and walked off. Gun's words irritated me on a different level. I knew he was with Saint, and they were fucking married, but it seemed I got my boxers in a twist over the fact Gun was close with Dusty. Like Tech and Quake. But also, everyone had to clue the hell in. I wouldn't fuck with Dusty's feelings. I wouldn't have started anything if I wasn't fully and completely serious about making her mine.

What I needed to calm the irritation was the woman who was currently covering her mouth as she laughed at something Henri said. Walking around the table, I took the chair Eve had just vacated and tugged her chair close. She let out a small squeal, but I reached out to steady her.

"Hi." She smiled.

Fuck. She was my future.

"Hey, darlin'." Reaching out, I ran the backs of my

fingers over her jaw while I used my thumb to gently trace her bottom lip. Her pupils shot wide.

"How can an innocent touch turn me on?" Henri's comment had Dusty choking on the air she sucked in sharply.

"Henri!" she scolded.

"Amour, you know I cannot help it. Now I know your man won't kill me, I like to push buttons to see how far I can go."

Smirking, I pinched her chin and leaned into her so I could kiss the corner to her mouth. Resting back, I caught Henri's amused gaze. "Henri, not sure how you thought you were safe around me. When did I give you that impression?"

Henri's gaze flared. "You... but... I am hers, so you can not hurt me, because Dusty will be upset."

"You got one thing wrong. You ain't hers. I am."

"Maverick," Dusty whispered. Her soft eyes held mine as she threaded our fingers together and brought my hand to her lap.

"Prez," Tech called from the table I'd left.

Catching Dusty's gaze, I lifted our joined hands and kissed the back of hers. "Be back in a sec."

"Okay." She smiled, and each one she shared with me was like the coolest breeze on a fucking hot day that relaxed you. Jesus, I sounded like a douche.

Shaking my head at myself, I made my way over to Tech and now Blaze. Blaze tipped back and forward on his feet with an excited gleam in his eyes. "Am I ever gonna get rid of you?" I asked him.

"No."

"You know if you deal any of your stupid shit outta this compound, I'll make you wish—"

"Yeah, yeah, all the threats in the world. I can't and won't do shit now you know my weakness."

He meant Henri. I didn't understand the connection they had, but it looked like it wasn't only sexual on Blaze's part.

Nodding, I turned to Tech. "What you got?"

"Jones."

"Who?"

"Fuckin' Officer Jones sent the message."

What the fuck? "Are you shittin' me?"

Tech laughed. "Not on this, Prez. We got the location just before the phone was destroyed. It was in his home residence."

"Fuck me. *That* I never expected."

"Might be good to have a cop on the inside," Blaze said. "You should make friends with him, find out why he was willing to warn you."

It would be good. It'd be the fucking best.

"We'd have to be damn discreet. No one can know we had a sit down with him." Lifting my gaze, I told Tech, "Have Wreck pay him a visit with one of our burner phones. We'll talk on the phone for now." Wreck was a big motherfucker, but he had skills of getting in and out undetected.

"I'll go talk to him now. Think he's in his room with Lucas." He started for the stairs. "Actually, I think I'll text him first." Tech veered off toward his room.

It left me alone with Blaze. "We would have helped you in the past."

Blaze tensed. "I know, but I didn't need it."

"Your business better not blow back on this club."

"As if he would let it." I took it the *he* was meant to be Henri when Blaze's gaze shot to him. "I'm getting out of it, but it'll take time."

"The help is there if you need it, as long—"

"As none of it touches the Diamond MC. I get it."

"Good," I grunted. "Never thought I'd see you turnin' yourself around for someone."

"Just takes that special someone, doesn't it?"

"It does." Guess us older guys could grow up eventually.

CHAPTER NINETEEN

Dusty

*M*averick sat beside me driving, but I couldn't take my gaze away from his hand on my thigh. We'd changed.

We'd become something more.

Yet I still couldn't believe we were an *us*, even with his hand on my leg. It was like a dream. One where your forever crush actually noticed you and asked you out. The constant wave of excitement that spread through me when I thought of Maverick was like a high without taking any drugs.

This was real.

It was happening.

He wanted me like I did him.

Even after everything I'd said. After waking in the

middle of the night screaming. After crying into his chest and admitting my weakness—how it could be good if I talked to someone about everything. He'd agreed and held me, talked to me until I drifted back asleep.

He hadn't mentioned my episode to me or when we went downstairs—in clothes I'd borrowed off Eve again. Though, when he'd seen West, he'd kissed my temple and said, "I'll grab the food. You go take a seat," and I'd watched as Maverick spoke quietly with West, whose eyes had widened before he started nodding. He also hadn't been intimidated by Adrik standing at West's back, glaring at Maverick with his arms crossed over his chest.

The one time I looked away, it was to see Torch and Quake walk in, and I'd missed Maverick slip into the kitchen. West and Adrik had headed my way.

When West took the seat opposite me, I'd given him a sad smile. "Did Maverick tell you I had a nightmare?"

"Who is Maverick? I do not know a Maverick. West, why are you—"

West's hand covered his husband's mouth. "Dear God, I love you, but stop. Maverick is Country's real name."

Adrik glared at West until he removed his hand. "Continue," he clipped.

They were honestly polar opposites, but I could see their love clearly in the way they looked at each other.

West had sighed, then smiled. "Country did mention it. You know what I went through." I did, and to this day, the thought of it still made me sick to the stomach. When I'd nodded, he went on, "Trauma comes in all different shapes and sizes. What's traumatic for some won't be for others and vice versa. I just want you to know that you have people you can talk to, me included, but if you want to see someone professional, I can suggest who I used to visit. It really helped, but again, it's not for everyone. If you feel talking to Country or Eve or me, anyone, helps, then do it. You aren't alone, sweetheart. Don't try and bottle anything because you're worried about being a burden or anything. You will never be, and your friends, your family, your man, all want to help you through this." His hand had slid across the table to take mine. "Don't hold anything in, okay?"

Tears had pricked my eyes, and I'd sniffed. "Thank you. I promise I won't keep it in."

I'd squeezed his hand, which he returned, and now, as I sat in the car, I felt like I needed to bring this up with Maverick.

My pulse raced so fast I could feel it tick in my neck. "Maverick?"

"Yeah, baby?"

"Thank you for having West talk to me."

His quick flash of eyes showed he appreciated my words. "I'd thought I'd fucked up."

"What? Why?"

His gaze went to his hand on my thigh. "You ain't touchin' me, darlin'. Noticed that when I reach out for you, you're willin' to touch me back in some way."

Quickly, I rested my hand over his. "Sorry, didn't mean to worry you. I… I just want you to know I may have nightmares, but the worry and fear from them evaporate when I wake up beside you."

"Fuck, baby," he groaned, his hand convulsing on my thigh. "Glad to hear I can bring you peace, darlin'."

"You always have."

He grinned again. "Dusty, maybe keep all the sweet for when I can kiss you after it, not while I'm drivin', yeah?"

Laughing, I nodded with a slight twinge to my cheek, but nothing I couldn't handle, thanks to Lucas and his pain meds. "Can I ask something?"

"Anythin'."

"I need to know… I think it would be better for me to know… the men who took me, the first time—"

"They'll never be a problem again."

I'd thought so. If not, I had a feeling Maverick would still be out there looking for them.

"Thank you, honey."

"I'll always protect you, Dusty, you know that, right?"

"I do." Completely.

"Good. Now, baby, before we hit your 'rents place, I

wanted to show you my house." He pulled up out front of a large modern townhouse. It wasn't anything like I pictured Maverick would have.

A finger tapped my nose, and he chuckled, and I realized I'd screwed it up when looking at his home. My face heated as I turned to him. "I'm so sorry. It's just not what I thought you would pick."

"No?"

I winced. "Sorry, that was really rude. I can't believe the things I do and say sometimes."

"Like wantin' me to plant my seed in you."

"Oh my God, can we not bring that up?"

His chuckle was low. "Fuckin' love the things you say and how you act." He nodded outside. "Come on, I'll show you around."

We got out of the car, and I started up the walk to the townhouse. "I really am sorry for—"

"Dusty."

I glanced back to see Maverick standing at the driver-side door. He thumbed across the road. "This is mine."

Across the street sat something very different from a townhouse. The light gray clapboard house sat on land bigger than any other around it. This house was totally country for my Country.

With a skip in my step, I met him at the front of the car and smacked him in the stomach. "That's for letting me think the other one was yours." I waved a hand at his house. "This is you. One hundred percent you."

When I looked up at him, my breath caught in my throat at the intensity. "I seriously fuckin' regret it took us this long, darlin'. You were made for me right from the damn start, and I didn't see it. I let my head run wild from past experiences, but I won't let that happen again. Dusty, a house is just a house, but now I've got you, I know it's somethin' more because eventually, it'll become a family home. *Our* family home."

Tears welled and fell. I pushed my forehead into Maverick's chest, wrapping my arms around him. "Honey," I whispered. "You can't be sweet when I'm still healing, and I can't kiss you like I want to."

I lifted my head to see his grin. "Yeah? How do you wanna kiss me, darlin'?"

"Like you're mine."

He groaned as he looked to the sky, muttering, "God, give me strength." When his eyes met mine, they near blew me across the street with how much heat was in them. "Baby, I ain't a romantic guy, and I seem to confess shit at inappropriate times, but I can't not tell you. I can't hold it in anymore, darlin'. I fuckin' love you, Dusty Reyes."

My throat thickened with the rush of emotions. "Maverick, I'll take you in any way you come, because I love you as you are."

His hands shook as they cupped my cheeks and

stepped close, so our chests touched. "We're gonna be good together, baby."

I shook my head. "We're going to be the best."

"Fuckin' right," he clipped against my mouth as he pressed a kiss there. "Christ. Come on, let me show you around." He took my hand and led me across the street. "Anythin' you don't like, we can change."

"Maverick, this is your house, I'm not—"

He spun fast. "What did I say, darlin'?"

"Sorry?"

"This'll be ours. You make it how you want it to be happy here."

Resting my free hand on his chest, I slid it up to cup the side of his neck. "I'm not changing anything because I know I'll like it. But I'm going to pay my way—"

"Dusty," he warned.

"Let me have the yard. The rest we can deal with at a later date, when I can help you be less stubborn."

His gruff laughter had me smiling and my chest feeling light. "Baby," he said against my mouth. "The yard is yours, and I look forward to you tryin' to make me less stubborn about that shit."

My smile had probably grown a little crazy with how happy I was feeling, but I didn't care.

IT WAS good to be right, and I had been when I said I knew I'd like Maverick's house. It was homey and comfortable with a splash of country life, and I couldn't wait to get my hands on the front and back yard. I already had plans running through my mind for both.

Only now we were stopping at my parents' house, and a sense of dread twisted my stomach. Dad I wanted to see, as long as he didn't try to get me to stay, but Rebecca, I didn't. However, as Maverick took my hand, strength filled me, and together we walked up to the front door.

"Baby, this is a fuckin' mansion."

"It is, but it was always too big and scary when I was on my own." Which had been a lot.

Maverick's jaw clenched, and he punched the doorbell hard enough it broke. "Fuck."

Laughing, I wrapped both my hands around his arm. "Don't worry about it. They can afford to get it fixed." He grinned down at me. "Thank you for coming with me."

"You're stuck with me, Dusty. We deal with the good, the bad, and the damn ugly shit together."

"I love the sound of that, but I'm not sure I'll ever get used to knowing you're mine, and I can freely do this." I slid a hand down and gripped his butt cheek.

His eyes hooded. "Get used to it. No matter where we are or who we're with, I'm yours. So anytime you need my attention, you take it."

My pulse wouldn't quit racing, near making me dizzy. "Love you," I whispered, my throat too clogged with more of those pretty emotions I felt for him.

A throat cleared, and I pulled my hand off Maverick's butt like it was on fire. "I wasn't doing anything," I blurted to my dad.

Dad hid his grin behind his hand while *my* man just threw his head back and laughed. He cupped the side of my neck, gently tugged me close, and kissed the top of my head, still laughing.

"Why don't you two come on in?" Dad shifted back and swept an arm out.

Maverick slipped his hand to my shoulder, and we walked in together. When we stopped inside the door, Maverick said, "Look, I'm gonna be straight here. Dusty's my world, so if you want to work on your relationship with her, it's gonna come with me. Not only that, but the brothers of the club think the world of her, so they're gonna have her back and won't let you or your wife cause her any type of harm. Even mentally."

Dusty's my world.

Dusty's my *world.*

How could he possibly keep getting better and better while making my body and heart and soul all swoony?

"I can accept anything because I see the way she's looking at you right now, and I know you're her world as well," Dad replied. Tears stung my eyes as I gazed up at Maverick. When he peered down at me, his eyes softened before he dipped and kissed my nose.

He turned back to Dad. "Good. Now that shit's outta the way, if your wife's home, I'd prefer you to tell her not to show her face while we're here. She upset Dusty yesterday."

Dear God, was he trying to kill me with all this macho sweetness?

"Rebecca is no longer living here."

My gaze swung to him. "What?"

Dad gave me a sad smile. "My father always drilled into me money and status were everything, but it's not when you see your daughter with cuts, bruises, and bandages on her. I knew when I walked out from seeing you that things had to change. You won't have to see Rebecca again. I'm cutting back my hours at work and won't be moving Jenni in until you have formally met her and got to know her. I'm beyond sorry for the way we treated you. I would like a chance at fixing our relationship, if you agree."

"Dad," I choked. He'd gotten a wake-up call, which had shocked him so much he'd made big changes in his life. "I'd like that."

Tears clouded his gaze. "Thank you."

"Can I hug you?" I asked, and I caught Maverick's frown. He didn't like I had to ask my father for a hug, but my parents had never been comfortable with showing affection.

Dad sniffed and glanced to Maverick, who dropped his arm from my shoulders. "I'd like that." Dad opened his arms, and I walked into him, wrapping mine around his waist. "Thank you," I whispered.

His grip tightened around me until Maverick clipped, "Not too tight, she's healin'."

Dad gave my cheek a quick kiss. "Don't thank me for things that should have happened all along."

Smiling, I nodded. "I'm just glad it's happening now."

He sniffed again and wiped at his face. "Me too." He cleared his throat. "I'll let you get your things. But would you two like to stay for dinner? I'm not a cook, like our usual one, who has the day off, but I can order food like a pro."

Looking up at Maverick, he winked. "I'm happy to do whatever you want, darlin'."

Smiling, I turned back to Dad. "We'd love to. Maybe… if you're comfortable with it, but you could come to family day at the compound. We have a big cookout."

"Your daughter's a fuckin' brilliant cook," Maverick added.

"I-I'd really like that."

Maverick chuckled and slapped Dad on the upper arm, which had Dad stumbling forward a little. "Relax, Liam, we ain't so bad once you get to know us, and you'll have to because Dusty ain't goin' anywhere from our lives."

Dad laughed nervously. "I look forward to getting to know everyone."

It seriously felt like I was floating up the stairs to my room. I didn't understand, and I wouldn't try to figure out how I could be so happy after everything. It was luck. It had to be.

CHAPTER TWENTY

Country

Sitting in my office, I waited for the phone call to come through with State, Death, and Wreck. Jones had texted the other day with a time after leaving it for a few days. The brothers were talking amongst themselves, but all I could do was lean back in the chair and think about Dusty. Christ, the last few days had been amazing. We'd stayed at my place the last couple of nights, where she'd assisted while I cooked dinner, and I couldn't explain the feeling it gave me right in the middle of my chest seeing her in my house and puttering around like she'd been made to do so. She'd talked enthusiastically about what she was dying to do to the yards, and, hell, her excitement had extended over to me. I couldn't wait to see her vision.

She'd had a dream the previous night, but not the one before, where she woke yelling and reaching out for something. As soon as it cleared, I tucked her close and held her, telling her about the shit I used to get up to in the past until she'd settled once again.

Every time I saw fear in her eyes, my gut clenched, not easing until she realized she wasn't back in the clinic with the men standing over her. But what cooled my blood and settled my stomach was how calm she appeared as soon as she knew I was at her side.

"Bet he's thinkin' about her," I heard Death mumble.

State hummed. "Yeah, can totally see it written on his face. What do you reckon, Wreck?"

Wreck grunted. "As long as they're happy."

Everyone looked at him.

"What?"

Death snorted. "Being with Lucas has softened you, brother."

Wreck glared. "So fuckin' what."

The phone rang, and I put it on speaker. "Country."

"How did you know it was me?" Jones asked, and he sounded a little pissed about the fact we'd found out. It was thanks to his call that we made the club extra clean before the cops ripped through it. The members were still putting shit back where it belonged.

"We have our ways."

"Blaze and your guy Tech."

"Why ask if you know?" I queried.

"Just wanted to be sure."

"Why did you warn me? Not many cops would go out of their way to do such a thing."

Jones sighed through the phone. "You didn't see me that night, but I was in the warehouse with Yano."

I shared a look with my brothers. "Why didn't you stop us?"

"Let's say the force didn't know I was on my own mission to get rid of Yano, but you took him. Is he gone?"

"I ain't sayin' shit—"

"I wouldn't have warned you if I was going to record your confession right now. I don't give a fuck if he's gone because at least there's one less fuckup out there in the world. Same as Donald Spring."

"They've been dealt with."

"Good. Look, I'm running my own show, but if I hear something about the club, I'll let you know."

"Why?" I clipped.

"Because it looks like you guys can do things I can't. There's corruption in the force. I'm not one to trust easily, but I've seen your actions concerning Dusty. She's safe. You've made sure of it while dealing with pricks who didn't deserve to breathe the same air as us. We can either work together or not. I don't care, but don't get in my way from getting to the bottom of who's buying my coworkers."

"Buying them how? What's so different from you informin' us about shit and what they're doin'?"

His laugh wasn't with humor. "A fucking big difference."

Looked like he wasn't going to trust us fully just yet, but he went out of his way to have our back. "Let us know if you need assistance in anythin'."

The room fell silent.

"I will," he finally said. "I'm not going to be able to keep this phone. Is there another way to contact you?"

"We'll get a small device to you. It has a camera that you can turn on and off, as well as an alarm."

"I'm guessing that whoever broke in the first time will leave it someplace for me?"

I glanced to Wreck; he nodded. "I'll leave it where you hid your house key."

Jones cursed. "How the fuck did you find that? And who is this?"

"Doesn't matter who it is. Just know the club and I are one. Trust me, you trust my brothers."

"Fine," Jones bit out before hanging up.

"Fuck me," I uttered. "Let's keep a close eye on the people Jones works with. I already don't trust that other cunt who mouthed off, and it looks like Jones doesn't either."

"What kind of shit are they dealin' in?" Death muttered.

"Whatever it is, it's got Jones on the outside of it all and willin' to help us out."

"Corrupt motherfuckers," State clipped. We already knew there were some in the force, from when they'd tried to set State up. But from what Jones was saying, there were more than a few.

"Wreck, get the brooch to his place. I'll have Tech *and* Blaze, since it doesn't look like we're gettin' rid of the dickhead, look into some shit. We'll help where we can."

"If he presses that emergency button, we're ridin' in to help?" Death asked with a smirk; he already knew the answer.

"We help those who help us."

"Agreed," State said.

Taking the burner phone, I placed it in my desk drawer and locked it. Standing, I nodded to the door. "Sounds like a party's happenin' instead of cleanin'."

State grinned. "A party while cleaning more like it."

"Looks like the prez wants to get back out to his woman." Death chuckled.

"Fuck off, brother," I bit out and opened the door. "Lock it when you leave," I called over my shoulder. The idiot had been right. I wanted to get out of there to see Dusty.

Dusty

EARLIER

Henri and I were in the kitchen cleaning up the mess the police left. I couldn't believe the sight when we'd got home. Why they needed to turn out all the drawers was beyond me. Thankfully, we'd been at it for a while and were making progress. Maverick had even called in most brothers and all club girls to help. Since Henri had arrived with Blaze, he decided to stay.

"Is it not a good time for us to talk about Blaze?" I asked, placing more cutlery into the dishwasher. If I hadn't taken over this job, Henri would have just put them in the drawer without washing them. Even though they'd been on the floor.

"Amour, I must tell you I do love this life for you. I have not been this entertained in a long time." He gasped and swung to me, clutching his chest. "I do not mean with you being kidnapped."

Rolling my eyes, I waved him off. I knew he would never mean that. "I know, Henri."

He sighed. "I do love coming here to see you, and I have now stolen your friends for my friends. I hope that's all right with you."

Smiling, I nodded. "It's fine because you're my friend too. But Henri, don't think I didn't notice your change in subject. Do I need to get you drunk to talk about Blaze?"

"I could use a drink." He lifted himself up to sit on the counter. "I found Blaze bleeding out in an alleyway one night. He did not want the police called, so I took him back to my house and patched him up. From then on, I couldn't get rid of him. We slept together many times. It wasn't until I found out about his... jobs that I called it quits. I hadn't seen him for years until I called him, using the number he'd left for me, to help with your situation."

Moving over to him, I rested against his thigh. "And now?"

"Now, I do not know. But it is hard to stay away from him."

"You've grown feelings again for him?"

"Non, they just never went away. He picked his jobs over me. I was never important."

"I don't think that's the case now."

Henri huffed. "I cannot be with someone who does what he does."

The doors to the kitchen swung open, and Eve entered but stopped when she took us both in. "Who do I need to hurt?"

It brought a smile to my face. "No one, well... yet. We're just talking."

"What about?" She made her way over and rested against the counter opposite us.

"About Blaze and me," Henri supplied. Eve rose a brow, and Henri ended up telling her about their past.

Eve grinned.

"Eve, I don't think it's something to smile about."

"I do, since I overheard talk about Blaze getting out of the business."

"What?" Henri breathed.

Eve nodded. "He spoke to Country about it. Said he was going to quit, but it'll take time to get out of the things he does." She tapped her chin. "I wonder why he would want out."

Hope for Henri filled me.

"Are you sure?" Henri asked.

"Yep," Eve said, popping the *p*.

Henri's wide gaze shot to me, to Eve, and back to me. Laughing, I asked, "Are you going to find him?"

His expression morphed into a bored one as he shrugged. "I do not run to him—"

The doors opened, and Blaze stepped in with Maverick. Henri jumped off the counter, ran right up to Blaze, and kissed him like he was his favorite lollipop.

Eve and I shared a look, laughing.

Blaze broke the kiss, his warm gaze running over Henri's face that he'd cupped. "We're going," he announced to the room before dragging Henri out.

Henri waved over his shoulder. "Au revoir."

Maverick placed his hands on his hips and watched them go with an amused smirk. When he looked back at me, his chin tipped up. "We're headin' to the house."

"But I haven't finished in here." I glanced around.

"Darlin', the best thing about being the president is that you have people do things you ask. I'm sending Quake in here to clean with Eve."

Eve groaned, but she saluted Maverick. "You got it, captain. Only can it be anyone but Quake?" Did Eve have a problem with Quake? Why?

"Nope."

The doors opened, and Quake stepped through. I caught Eve's scan over his body and realized why she didn't want Quake around. She was attracted to him, though you wouldn't guess it since she quickly glared at him.

"Have fun, you two," I said with a smile as I walked over to Maverick, who was holding his hand out for me. As soon as I took it, he placed a soft kiss against the corner of my mouth.

When I looked back, Eve shot me the finger but did so with a grin. Quake winked before he got to cleaning.

Glancing up at Maverick, I wrapped my other hand around his arm and told him, "I do feel guilty for leaving."

"Don't. You're still healin'. Everyone knows it."

"Okay." I couldn't argue with that. "I need to grab my bag before we leave." The thought of sleeping at Maverick's tickled my stomach.

"Already got it." Maverick grinned.

On the drive to his house, Maverick shared with me about the warning from Officer Jones and then the phone call.

"Just to be safe, darlin', if anyone tried to pull you over or take you to the police station, ask for Jones."

I squeezed his hand. "Okay, I will."

"Not that I'll let you outta my sight outside of the compound."

"Maverick." I started to laugh, but when he didn't join in, I gulped it back. "You're serious?"

"Until we know what's goin' on, yeah."

"Maverick, honey, no one will try and take me again."

"Baby, just for a little while, I need you to humor me and do as I ask. If I'm not around when you wanna do something down the street, take some brothers or even Eve. Never alone. Okay?"

"All right," I said instantly, because I never, until that moment, realized what Maverick had gone through when I'd been taken. It had scared him. *Really* scared him. Not wanting to put him through that again, I would do as asked.

"I'm going to quit at the clinic, and Henri wants me to come on full-time when I go back to work."

His shoulders sagged as if a weight just lifted off them. He brought my hand up to kiss the back of it. "Good. I'll work out a security system for Henri's that's connected to Death's, so we can keep an eye on things."

"Blaze has probably already set something up for him."

"Maybe, I'll check with him. But you ain't goin' back for a couple of weeks, right?"

"I mean, I could be okay for next week."

"We'll see."

"I'll go insane with boredom," I warned.

"I'll buy books, get Netflix, and any video game you want."

"Well, maybe I could take two weeks off. As long as you can spend as much time with me as possible."

"Deal, darlin'."

"But you know I'll be happy here at the house or even at the compound. Both are homes to me."

"I know, Dusty, and I'm fuckin' lucky you are who you are."

My heart stumbled. "What's that?"

"Perfect for me."

Thinning my lips, which Maverick saw, I dipped my brows and said, "Maybe us spending a lot of time together isn't a good thing. Especially if you say sweet things like that, and I can't have my mouth on you in the ways I want."

"You're right. Let's not talk at all. Fuck, don't even look at me."

Laughing, I leaned over and kissed his shoulder. God, this man made me happy.

EPILOGUE

Dusty

*J*f anyone asked me what the biggest pain in the butt was, my current answer would be having a patient man who didn't want to hurt me if we actually had sex.

I missed sex with him.

I *wanted* sex with him.

But he'd kept his picture-worthy penis away from me for five damn weeks.

"Will you quit thinkin' about dick and kill that guy?" Quake bumped my shoulder, and I quickly pressed the buttons on the controller to do so.

"But seriously, Quake," I started, and he groaned, dropping his head back on the couch. I ignored him and went on, "My face feels fine, and I've told him this, but he won't, *you know*, with me."

"Do I have tits?" Quake asked.

I looked. "No. Though, you are looking a little saggy there—"

"Hold your fuckin' tongue, Dusty. I ain't saggy anywhere."

"Uh-huh," I teased. "But back to me—"

"No. No. No." Quake dropped the controller on the couch in his room at the compound and stood. "Adore you, sister, but I don't have a pussy. I ain't one of your girls. I will never in this lifetime talk to you about fuckin' my prez or why he won't do you. Understand?" He pointed toward his door. "Go and ask him or, hell, jump him."

Rolling my eyes, I sighed. "Fine, I'll go ask Tech."

"Yes." He clapped. "Do that and tell him Quake sent you."

"Do you know where Tech is?" I asked, standing.

"Right here, babe." Tech appeared in the doorway. "What's up?"

Quake's eyes widened. "For the love of God, don't ask that."

"Quake suggested I jump Maverick since he's still being careful with me."

Tech's head tilted in thought. "Reckon that'll work."

Glancing to Quake, I waved my hand toward Tech.

"See, that's how you could have told me. In a calm manner."

Quake ran his hands over his face. "Jesus, I need a drink."

"Yo, Tech," we heard called, and a smile came over me. "You seen Dusty?"

"Yeah, Prez, she's right here." Tech pointed in Quake's room.

Quake suddenly grabbed my arm and dragged me out of his room. When he saw Maverick, he tugged me the few steps it took to stop in front of my man. "Here. Take her." Quake shoved me at Maverick, who smirked.

"What you done now, darlin'?"

Quake's eyes widened. "No," he yelled and covered his ears with his hands as he walked back into his room, slamming the door after himself.

Laughing, I shook my head. "He really is such a baby."

"You didn't talk about your uterus again?"

Laughing harder, all I could think of was how much fun I'd had telling Quake my version of why women got their periods and how they could make them cranky. When I'd mentioned how a woman's body discarded the monthly buildup of the lining of our uterus, I thought he was about to pass out. He'd even swayed on his feet a little.

"Not this time."

He curled an arm around my shoulders and walked

us downstairs after I waved to Tech. Maverick nodded to him before he went into Quake's room.

"Pap smears?" Maverick asked.

"Damn, I forgot I was going to explain about those."

Maverick chuckled. "You're a devil in disguise. The brothers will quit talkin' to you altogether soon."

"If they try, I'll show them videos of a woman giving birth."

Maverick shuddered. "You really are evil."

"Only a little."

"Dusty," Henri called from where he sat on Blaze's lap at a table with Eve, Courtney, State, Adrik, and West. "Come here."

Maverick pulled me around to face him. Looking up, I asked, "You okay?"

"Darlin', it's your choice. You can either go hang with them, or we could go to our room here or to home. What do you want?"

A ballerina danced her way around inside of my stomach. "If I say to the bedroom here, will we be doing anything?"

He watched as he brushed the back of his hand over my nearly healed cheek. When his gaze locked back on mine, my knees trembled at the heat I saw there.

"You want somethin' from me, baby?"

"Yes. Dear God, yes, please."

He chuckled. "Tell me what you want from me."

Placing my hands on his hips, I rested my chin on his chest. "How about I show you?"

His jaw clenched. "I can take you home for privacy—"

"No. Here, where it all started for us."

"Fuck, baby," he clipped and took my hand, leading me back to the stairs.

We heard Henri say loudly, "I don't think she's coming over here." There were a couple of snorts and chuckles in reply. I didn't care that they knew we were going to the bedroom. It didn't worry me they probably knew we were going to have sex. All I worried about was getting Maverick to the bedroom quickly. Which was why I overtook him on the stairs and pulled him down the hall, listening to his throaty chuckle.

Once in the bedroom, I pushed him toward the bed and turned to close and lock the door. When I faced him, my mouth dried at the beauty before me.

Maverick had taken off his vest and tee. He stood in only jeans with the top button undone.

How was I so lucky to have such a fine man be all mine?

I didn't know, but I would take him, cherish him, and hold on tight to him.

My heart raced in my chest, my nipples pebbled, and even my pussy throbbed. Finally, I was going to get some from the man who was all mine but who'd also been my obsession for two years.

"Maverick," I whispered.

"Baby, you got too many clothes on."

I cocked a brow. "If I get undressed, you won't go easy on me, right? We are going to have sex?"

He smirked. "That's the plan."

"Right." I whipped off my top and undid my bra. Sliding it down my arms, I threw it to the floor. "Good, great, can't wait." I pushed my shorts to the floor along with my panties and kicked off my flip-flops. When I straightened, it was to find Maverick right in front of me, grinning.

"Fuckin' love you."

"Love you more; now give me your cock."

He laughed. "I'm startin' to think you like me just for my cock."

"Honey." I curled my arms around his shoulders and jumped, wrapping my legs around his waist as his hands landed on my ass, holding me close. "I love you more than anything in the world. But, babe, I need you inside me like I need air to breathe."

"Christ," he grunted and slanted his mouth over mine. Gone was the sweet press of lips, gone the gentle touches. He gripped me to him like he was made to wear me, and we kissed, all tongue, teeth, and nips. My cheek may have twinged a little, but I didn't care. I'd missed him even when he'd been at my side.

Breaking the kiss, our panting mingled. "Lucas put an IUD in me—"

"What the fuck is that, and do I need to kill him?"

Smiling like a maniac, I patted his shoulder. "It'll keep me from getting pregnant."

"For now?"

My stomach swooshed. "Yeah, for now."

"Good. I've always used protection… until now."

"Good. Bed or wall?"

He didn't laugh that time. His heated gaze seared me as he pressed my back against the wall. "Fuck, now I don't know. Wanna eat you, but wanna fuck you."

Slipping a hand between us, I unzipped him and pulled his hard cock free. "We can do all that later after we have shower sex, but that's after our wall sex."

His hands tightened on my ass, his jaw clenching again, and he dropped his head to my shoulder, groaning when I rubbed the tip of his cock against my entrance.

"Honey," I whispered, dropping my head back to hit the door as he slowly pushed inside me. "God, yes."

Maverick licked up my neck and bit my earlobe. His breath turned heavy when he growled, "Fuckin' mine."

"Yes, honey. All yours."

He hummed under his breath and pulled out just as slow. "Fuck."

I gripped his shoulders. "More, please."

He grunted. "Anything for you, sugar." His palms readjusted on my ass, and then, hell… then he was *fucking* me. His hips pistoned in and out. His thick cock filled and unfilled me like he was the perfect fit. When his teeth latched onto my neck and sucked, I cried out, "Yes," and moaned when he dipped and took a nipple into his mouth.

My body buzzed. I blinked, unseeing as the orgasm built within my lower stomach. It was there but just out of reach. Still, it had me shivering and tingling.

"Jesus fuck, darlin'." Maverick pushed me into the wall harder and removed a hand from my ass to grip my chin. He forced my head down so he could claim my mouth like he was my body.

"Oh, God, yes," I cried. Toes curled, fingers dug into his skin, and I rode up and down on his cock through a climax that had me seeing stars.

Maverick groaned, kissing me hard. He tensed for a second, then fucked me faster, shooting his cum into me while I drank down his grunts.

When he pulled back, I dropped my head to his shoulder, trying to catch my breath. His hand shifted my hair, and he planted a kiss on my exposed skin. "Love you, Dusty."

I moaned when he shifted and took us to the bed. He slipped free, and I could feel the gush of his cum escaping. Lifting my head, I cupped his cheek. "Thank you for making my life a good one."

"Darlin'."

"No, you have. You've accepted my love and given me yours. Forever."

He pressed his forehead against mine. "Forever. It won't always be perfect, but we'll always make it work."

"We will."

I couldn't picture my life without him in it, and since I didn't and probably wouldn't scare him off with some of the things that ran through my mind, I knew he saw the same for me.

We'd always been each other's.

ACKNOWLEDGMENTS

Thank you, reader, for taking a chance on this new MC series. Country has always been in the background of my mind since I started the Polished P & P series. I knew he would eventually want his own story, and good news, he won't be the only one. So far, Death, Torch, Tech, and Quake will be getting their own books, but I'm just not sure when.

As always, a big thanks goes to Becky and her team at Hot Tree Editing for their help and hard work in deciphering my mistakes.

Another massive thank you goes to Christian at Cover by Christian for his amazing design work for the cover, I look forward to working with you in the future! And to Wander for the perfect photo of Jonny!

To my family: Craig, Shayla, and Jake, thank you for your constant support. More importantly, to Shayla who has helped me by working out the family tree and timeline for this series. I'm so glad you've turned eighteen and can enjoy my work as much as you do. Though, you need to quit pestering me for more books 😉

For my main beta ladies, Lindsey, Rachel (my amazing sister), Miranda, Amanda Berry and Amanda Evans, thank you for everything you do!

Lastly, my appreciation goes to Social Butterfly PR, it's been a pleasure working with you Sarah!

ALSO BY LILA ROSE

Hawks MC: Ballarat Charter

Holding Out (Free)

Outplayed (standalone related to the Hawks MC)

Climbing Out

Finding Out (novella)

Black Out

No Way Out

Coming Out (m/m novella)

Out to Find Freedom (standalone related to the Hawks MC)

Hawks MC: Caroline Springs Charter

The Secret's Out

Hiding Out

Down and Out

Living Without

Walkout (novella)

Hear Me Out (m/m)

Break Out (novella)

Fallout

Out of the Blue (standalone related to the Hawks MC: m/m/m)

Out Gamed (standalone related to the Hawks MC: novella)

Hawks MC: Next Generation

Coyote

Ruin (m/m)

Polished P & P series (m/m romance)

Wreck Me Forever

Never a Saint

Working Out West

Diamond MC

Country

Romantic Comedies

Making Changes

Making Sense

Fumbled Love

Bumbled Love

Trinity Love Series

Left to Chance (m/m/f novel)

Love of Liberty (m/m/f novella)

Standalones

In The Dark (paranormal)

Havoc's Mate (paranormal novella)

Senseless Attraction (Y / A)

Titles under L. Rose

The Hidden Kingdom Trilogy

(reverse harem romance)

A Torn Paige

A Lost Paige

A Final Paige

www.ingramcontent.com/pod-product-compliance
Lightning Source LLC
Chambersburg PA
CBHW070116120726
47909CB00002B/625